Titles by *Langaa* RPC...

John Nkemngong Nkengasong
Letters to Marions (And the Coming Generations)

Amady Aly Dieng
Les étudiants africains et la littérature négro-africaine
d'expression française

Tah Asongwed
Born to Rule: Autobiography of a life President

Frida Menkan Mbunda
Shadows From The Abyss

Bongasu Tanla Kishani
A Basket of Kola Nuts

Fo Angwafo III S.A.N of Mankon
Royalty and Politics: The Story of My Life
Basil Diki
The Lord of Anomy

Churchill Ewumbue-Monono
Youth and Nation-Building in Cameroon: A Study of
National Youth Day Messages and Leadership Discourse
(1949-2009)

**Emmanuel N. Chia, Joseph C. Suh & Alexandre
Ndeffo Tene**
Perspectives on Translation and Interpretation in
Cameroon

Linus T. Asong
The Crown of Thorns
No Way to Die
A Legend of the Dead: Sequel of *The Crown of Thorns*
The Akroma File
Salvation Colony: Sequel to *No Way to Die*

Vivian Sihshu Yenika
Imitation Whiteman

Beatrice Fri Bime
Someplace, Somewhere
Mystique: A Collection of Lake Myths

Shadrach A. Ambanasom
Son of the Native Soil
The Cameroonian Novel of English Expression: An
Introduction

**Tangie Nsoh Fonchingong and Gemandze John
Bobuin**
Cameroon: The Stakes and Challenges of Governance and
Development

Tatah Mentan
Democratizing or Reconfiguring Predatory Autocracy?
Myths and Realities in Africa Today

Roselyne M. Jua & Bate Besong
To the Budding Creative Writer: A Handbook

Albert Mukong
Prisonner without a Crime: Disciplining Dissent in
Ahidjo's Cameroon

Mbuh Tennu Mbuh
In the Shadow of my Country

Salvation Colony

Sequel to *No Way to Die*

Linus T. Asong

Langaa Research & Publishing CIG
Mankon, Bamenda

Publisher:
Langaa RPCIG
Langaa Research & Publishing Common Initiative Group
P.O. Box 902 Mankon
Bamenda
North West Region
Cameroon
Langaagrp@gmail.com
www.langaa-rpcig.net

Distributed outside N. America by African Books Collective
orders@africanbookscollective.com
www.africanbookscollective.com

Distributed in N. America by Michigan State University Press
msupress@msu.edu
www.msupress.msu.edu

ISBN: 9956-558-94-X

© Linus T. Asong 2009
First Published in 2006 by Patron Publishing House,
Bamenda, Cameroon

DISCLAIMER

The names, characters, places and incidents in this book are either the product of the author's imagination or are used fictitiously. Accordingly, any resemblance to actual persons, living or dead, events, or locales is entirely one of incredible coincidence.

Contents

Part One

Part Two

Part One

Chapter One

Dr. William Eshuonti

When I picked up the receiver and looked across at the clock on the wall, the time was exactly 11 p. m, on Wednesday, the 10th day of the month of May, 1971. May is traditionally the cruellest month of the rainy season. It was so unpredictable. It could begin with scorching sunshine early in the morning, deceive you into washing your dirty clothes and bedding, or into planting your crops in the garden or leave for the farm without an umbrella. And then an hour or two later it would turn into a deluge for hours.

Some years the rains began so heavily in April that farmers rushed into their farms to plant. And then with only a brief rainfall in early May, the rest of the month would witness not a single drop more. May 1971 was such a month. Although rain had been expected for weeks, thick clouds gathered in the horizon every afternoon, but dissipated by the evening without as much as a shower. The weather on such occasions was unbearably hot.

"Willie, you may not know what has happened," Dr. Essemo began.

"Until you tell me," I responded. Dr. Essemo's breathing was fast and he spoke with a voice that contradicted the repose air I had always attributed to him.

"What is it, boss?"

"That your albatross..." he began

"Mr. Dennis?" I asked immediately.

"Yes," he answered.

3

"What is he up to this time?"

"He tried to hang himself a few minutes ago."

"You don't mean it. Found him with a rope near a tree or something?" It sounded bizarre in my ears.

"He has just been removed from under the roof of my boys' quarters where he lived. The roof broke when he hung on it and fell on him. But for that I would be sending funeral messages across the country now."

"You say ashia they leave the kenja for ya hand," I mused. "So where is he?" I then inquired.

"Right here in the compound. The place is full. Too bad." I could hear Dr. Essemo transfer the receiver from one hand to the other.

I did not say anything for some time, and then I said:

"I will be there soon."

***

Dr. Essemo did not leave the main house until he heard me drive in. I must not have taken more than thirty minutes to arrive because I was anxious to see for myself what had happened.

"Where is Dr. Essemo?" I asked as soon as I got out of my car.

"Upstairs," somebody told me.

"Where is the corpse? Where is the Dennis?"

I could not wait for an answer because I could see a crowd that had gathered to the back of the building just in front of the Boys' Quarters. There must have been about fifty persons, for many kept coming while others were leaving.

The crowd made way for me as I approached. They all knew me as a good friend to Dr. Essemo.

Mr. Dennis Nunqam was sitting on a mound like a bundle of excrement on a rock, a long rope hanging round his neck. His head was lowered in shame, his hair dishevelled, his shirt torn in front and behind, and there were bruises on his right shoulder. The left leg of his trousers was torn from the knee to the ankle. He was shoeless, and sat with his hands clasped between his knees.

"Terrible," I exclaimed. "Absolutely terrible," I found myself repeating, bending down and giving Dennis a very long considering look. His eyes were dark and distraught, ghastly even, his lips bleeding.

Dr. Essemo heaved a long disconsolate sigh.

"I always told you that there was something the matter with this man," I said before recalling that I could be making the matter worse. "Now you will begin to believe me. See the trouble into which he has almost dragged us."

"And the swine was not going alone," Dr. Essemo said. "He had his two children with him."

"What?" I shouted.

Dr. Essemo grinned.

"How did the children get involved? I thought you said the family was in Mbongo?" I asked.

"The wife came in this afternoon," Dr. Essemo said, "with their two children which he wanted to *suicide*, along with himself."

"So where are the children?" I asked.

"Upstairs," Dr. Essemo said. "They are o.k.," he reassured me. "I've checked them. As God would have it, the upper and lower edges of the bed in which they had been lying when the cow tried to hang himself caught part of the crumbling roof that might have hurt them."

I felt hurt, severely hurt. "Listen to me, Dr. Max," I warned in a fit of fury. "Anybody who thinks of taking away his own life can just as easily take yours away. Whatever bond of friendship lies between the two of you, cut it off, right now. He leaves this house, now, for good, or else I'll hang him myself. There's no way you'll invite a nonentity to come and take control of your life. No way," I shouted.

Even before I finished talking I had started moving towards Dennis. Nobody knew what I planned to do. When I got to Dennis squatting in the grass I seized the rope round his neck and began to drag the miserable idiot towards a near-by tree. There was an outburst of laughter in spite of the macabre scene, as Dennis fought to pull me back.

"I want to show you how people hang," I said, pulling the swine until he screamed in pain.

"Leave him to die on his own," somebody pleaded.

There was a sudden flash of lightening across the dark sky, then a rumbling of thunder, followed by heavy drops of rain. The crowd dispersed instantly. Dr. Essemo returned with a knife and, cutting off the rope from Dennis' neck, left him sitting in the drizzle.

***

As we mounted the staircase into his sitting room, I remarked that I was not sure I had seen Gertrude. "She too has hanged herself?" I asked jokingly.

Dr. Essemo smiled fatiguely.

"You may think you are joking," he said. "You will never see her in this house again."

I could sense my brows crease. I was bewildered.

"Yes," Dr. Essemo nodded. "I had told you a few things I knew about her which she did not think I knew. I have finally told her my mind, all of it. And I can assure you it is all over."

"What provoked all that? That albatross?"

"Well, not quite."

"Then why had it to happen only in this particular context?" I inquired.

"It needed to happen someday some time down the line. I have called the whole thing off. My mind is made up," he declared.

6

I stood back and stared into the eyes of Dr. Essemo who suddenly looked small and contemptible to me.

"Dr. Essemo," I began, "you throw away a relationship you have spent the best years of your life building, all because of an idiot who cannot even wash his pants?" I shook my head bitterly.

"It is more serious than you think, doc. I now know that I have laboured in vain. None of the children in this house is mine."

"How do you mean?"

"When Gertrude was leaving this house, she took Viola's hand. I ordered her to leave my daughter behind."

"And then? She is as much her child as she is yours, so she could also want to be with her..."

"Listen to what she said, doc., 'Can you deliver a child as beautiful as this?" she asked me. 'Leave Bakru's child alone,' she told me."

"Bakru?"

"Bakru, Willie, Bakru my driver," he said with a terrible bitterness and sighed a heavy sigh that grated strangely in the quiet room.

I, in turn heard myself draw in a very long breath, unconsciously put my left thumb to my mouth and gnawed at the finger nail. It was as if the midnight air was pressing ominously on both our lungs. Like two lizards frozen into immobility in the dark of night we stared speechlessly and almost childishly into each other's eyes.

Chapter Two

Dr. Maximillian Essemo Aleukwinchaa

I decided that Manda Chabeule, Dennis' wife should spend the night with her children up in the visitors' room. I myself went into my room. After having served myself a full glass of whisky to clear my head, I threw myself on one of the sofas. I unbuttoned my shirt and trousers, placed my right hand under my head on the chair and stretched my shoeless feet on the small central table.

I fell asleep just for a few minutes when I sank into the chair. Thereafter, sleep vanished, even though my eyes remained closed, my mind and thoughts were robbed of coherence. I reflected on all my efforts time and money wasted. Thank God it had not ended the way the villain had hoped. How was I ever to clear myself? How were people, prone to misinterpretation as they are, ever going to understand precisely what had transpired between my friend and me?

That was the last favour I was going to render anybody on earth. Whatever else happened to Dennis thereafter, I said to myself, that was entirely his business. The world would forgive me and sympathize with me. Dennis could go to hell. If he hung himself anywhere else thereafter, it would be no fault of mine. God had prevented the idiot from dragging my reputation down in mud.

It was while I lay turning up these thoughts in my mind that I heard a timid knock on the door. That must have been an hour or so since I got into the room.

It was so timid a knock that I was sure it must be either Gertrude, or Manda. When I rose to the door and threw it open, I saw the monster! How he had succeeded in doing so with a half-broken spinal cord and a bruised skull, his left eye wounded and swelling even as I looked at it, and his knees definitely numb with pain and injury, I could not tell. But, apparently taking advantage of the fact that in the ensuing confusion I had left the main door to the building open, the cow had staggered and clambered up the staircase, had pushed the parlour door open, staggered across the sitting room to my door.

"How did you get in here?" I queried furiously.

"Doctor, the door was open," Dennis said, a thin line of blood running from below his left eye and disappearing under his chin. I noticed the wound, but couldn't care less.

"And so?" I shouted relentlessly.

"And so I came in..."

"What for?"

"Doctor, I came in here to beg for forgiveness for what I have done."

I gnawed at my lips, clenched and unclenched my fists and braced myself up as if to blow out the brains of the ass. Some unknown force held me back. The corpse might actually die in my hands, I thought and feared! Still fuming with virulent anger I pulled the ox by the collar of his shirt and spat out:

"You are coming to ask for forgiveness now because God has not allowed you to die in my house. If that roof had not come down, you would have been dead by now, and Maximillian Essemo Alekwinchaa would have been at the police station to answer questions concerning a poor miserable friend I have spent a fortune trying to help find his feet on this planet. Maximillian Essemo Aleukwinchaa would by now have become the subject of much malicious discussion, the laughing stock of the town.

"By some miracle I have been spared that embarrassment. And you are here to ask me to forgive you. I must be the greatest fool on this earth to listen to you. The only person who may have the patience to listen to you is God. And even God himself, I am not so sure will listen. Now you get your smelling anus out of this house before I do to you what you wanted to do for yourself."

So saying I seized the pig with my left hand by the shoulder of his torn shirt and, grabbing him with my right hand behind his neck, pushed him away violently across the parlour and shut my door.

***

Manda Chabeule

Here was me sitting on the bed in the visitor's room. My two sons were sleeping peacefully, but I myself, could I sleep? The thought of what my husband had just done was *choking* my heart as if somebody had poured broken bottles into my belly. If my husband did not like to continue to live with Dr. Max, why not return to Mbongo, why not escape to Mbongo? Why kill himself in the house of somebody who had done so much for my family? And even if he was determined to die, why die with my only two children? That kind of bad luck I have never seen in my life.

As I sat turning all these painful thoughts in my mind, I thought I heard a "kwa kwa" on the door. Who else could it be but Dr. Max, I asked myself. I rose and went to the door. It must be Dr. Max coming to give me ashia and to feel sorry for me. I wiped my eyes very quickly and pulled the door open without even asking who was there.

11

It was that satan they called my husband, Dennis
Nunqam Ndendemajem! I banged the door so loud that Dr.
Max came out. When I heard Dr. Max open his door I opened
my own door again and asked:

"Dennis, what do you want here? You want to come and
hang all of us?"

"I have come to ask for forgiveness, Manda..." he said
inside his throat.

"I am not God," I said to him. "Only God will ask you
what you have done. Only God will pay you."

"Have I not asked you to leave my house?" Dr. Max
asked and then pulling Dennis by the sleeve of his shirt
dragged him down the staircase, opened the door and threw
him outside like an old rag. Then I heard him telling the
watchnight:

"I see this man in this compound again, I shall hang the
two of you. And I mean every word of what I am saying."

As I looked through the window from the parlour I saw
the watchnight holding the hand of Dennis and pulling him
away. Dennis was not walking straight. It looked like he
had broken one of his legs. And then he was not even
refusing to go. When he got outside the gate the man locked
it after him and returned to his small house near the gate. I
said "Wheh, is that how the world is?"

I did not know where Dennis was going to that night.
Something said I should ask Dr. Max to ask him to come
back. In fact, I thought that after he had gone away for
sometime Dr. Max would send somebody to call him back.
He did not, and that too made me hate Dennis more and
more for what he had done. I was too angry with him to
mind at all.

Chapter Three

Dennis Nunqam Ndendemajem

I crossed the road from Dr. Essemo's gate, not knowing whether I was dead or alive. As I walked it felt as if I was walking thorns. After every few steps I looked back, expecting that Dr. Essemo would call me back. I could not understand that the same man who had come all the way to Mbongo to look for me, the same man who had spent so much time and money on me would turn me out of the house at that late hour, knowing that I knew nobody in the neighbourhood. As I walked away and as I listened in vain for somebody to call me back, I began to feel the weight of what I had really done. That was when I began to see that what I had done was very bad.

The house was gradually disappearing into the night behind me. This was the same house into which I had entered from a Mercedes, I thought; The same house in which I had been introduced to all its occupants as "the second master." I was now leaving it like a pig that nobody wanted to see. That feeling alone drove the pains away from my bones for a long time.

At first I walked up towards the town, and then I saw one or two people. Then I recalled that many of the people who had come to shame me in the compound had come from the north, to the right side of the GRA as you left Dr. Essemo's residence.

I would not go that way and bring more disgrace on to myself. I would go south, to the left, even if God lived to the north. In fact, had I gone north to the city and not south away from metropolitan Menako, I would have found many churches within an hour.

Southwards, there were very few houses, mostly gardens, tennis courts, swimming pools. I staggered downwards. Twenty minutes later, I saw flashes of lightening, heard thunder rumbling from all sides, and then felt drops of rain. There was no house near-by, the kind into which I could enter, for the compounds were all heavily fenced. Even if they were not fenced, I could not enter any house because I was sure that Dr. Essemo must have telephoned everybody to warn them not to receive me.

I took shelter under a eucalyptus tree. I leaned, head down, not even feeling the rain that poured mercilessly down on me until it ceased a bit. I Then went back into the road and continued my painful downward trek.

It was a full kilometre from Dr. Essemo's house to the main road, but I made it, in spite of the severe pain. A certain force, mysterious, and irresistible, seemed to impel me, seemed to tell me to go on, that my fortune or rather my future, if there was ever going to be any such thing, now lay not behind me with Dr. Essemo, but forward in the unknown.

But the unperturbed forward movement was dictated more by the fierce soreness in my body than by anything mysterious! It was impossible for me to turn left, right, or even sit down and rise again, even if I wanted to. My neck, back, knees, elbows and ankles ached as though a thousand needles had been drilled into every millimetre of my flesh.

It was thus safer to keep going - to continue standing or moving erect, if I had been moving or standing, or to continue sitting down if I had been sitting. I would keep going until my ailing feet could carry me no more. And then, I would go down and lie there, for as long it lasted. Like the robot that I had finally become, I wandered mechanically on, lifting and throwing one leg after the other.

I finally reached the high way. I turned southwards again and wobbled on. It must have been nearly 3 o'clock in the morning. Somebody, going either up or down, would have to meet me. What would I tell such a person if he wanted to know what had happened to me. I needed to prepare to defend myself. Was I going to say I had just survived a suicide attempt and that I had been driven away from the house? How could I do that?

That I was looking for God was true. But that did not mean that I was totally ignorant of the Bible. If I could remember nothing else, I certainly remembered the story of the rich man who was travelling from Jericho to Jerusalem when he fell into the hands of thieves. They beat him and robbed him, and left him wounded. Yes, I had an answer to any such question.

Apparently nature was following my innermost thoughts because presently I thought I heard a noise behind me as though somebody was rolling down a motor tyre. Then a faint light seemed to accompany the noise, projecting my thin shadow in front of me. I could not turn to find out what it was, so I stood, almost in the centre of the road. Then a bicycle rode past me.

"Helep, pa," I yelled. "I die. Thieves have killed me!"

The rider rode a few meters ahead of me, moved to the road side, stopped and looked back. I trudged down until I reached him.

"Who be you?" the rider asked.

"Dennis Nunqam Ndendemajem. I work for the Central Cooperatives Agency in Mbongo."

"Whas matter that you look so?"

"I came to see my brother who works with the church of God down this way," I began rather hesitantly. "We had many breakdowns, and so reached late. I am new in this town. When the lorry went away, thieves attacked me, beat me and took away everything."

The rider descended from his bicycle, and pointed his torch at my face to confirm the story.

"Sorry, sa. Them really do you."

I grunted, praying that he should not turn out to be somebody who had heard of what nearly happened to me.

"So I do how?" the rider asked.

I was silent, and, in fact, I did not really know what to ask from him. The pain was obvious in my face.

"You know any church here?" I asked. If I had to talk to God I must first find a church.

"Nealest chursh na AKA," the rider said. He then introduced himself as "Matty, or Mathias, tapper."

I was temporarily relieved. "Thieves," I said. "Thieves held me, tied my hands and neck and took away everything I had. Everything. Everything," I repeated.

"Everything? Where you were going to?"

"Down down there. I say I was going to see my brother who works near the church."

"Which chursh?"

"Pardon me, pa, they have beaten me so much that I cannot think properly. Is there no church down this way. No church of God? No place where one can ....?" I almost said "a place where one can ask God for forgiveness," but thought it would be stupid.

The tapper got off his bicycle, adjusted the two calabashes that hung one on each side, made it stand on its own and came closer to me. He took out a torch from a multi-coloured raffia bag that hung by his side and pointed the light flush into my face.

"Vely sorly, man. They really do you-eh!" he said. He pointed the torch down my body and shook his head sadly.

"For chursh, I know one is down down there," the tapper resumed. "AKA, they call it. But you know even if your brother work in church, he cannot fit be there now. Whas is the name of the chursh you said he work for?"

16

Why would I mention the name of a church I did not know? I decided to go back to his own answer. "The one you just called," I said. "You say it is what?"

"Aka."

"Yes," I nodded. I needed a church, that was all. And I needed one as soon as possible. I needed to communicate with God at once. "My brother works there," I kept on with my lies. "Church of God..."

Pa Matty was not going that far. "But I go take you near for there," he offered. "You go have to manage for this my Mercedes," the man added with a touch of humour.

I was very grateful but could not smile back. My entire face was frozen and the muscles taut with agonizing pain.

"Thank you very much," I responded. It took about thirty minutes before we finally took off because I could not lift myself onto the bicycle on my own. And each time the man tried to help me on the entire front part of the bicycle rose. On one of the attempts he almost lost a calabash. A solution was found when the man pushed the bicycle to the edge of the road, climbed on it and asked me to manage to climb on a stone and throw my right leg over the back seat.

Chapter Four

Dennis Nunqam Ndendemajem

About two kilometres down the road I noticed that the man kept sniffing as if something was smelling him. It was then that I came to myself and became aware that there was a bundle of excrement under the pants I was wearing, a result of the impact of the attempt to hang myself.

"I beg, sir, when you see a small stream," I implored him, "please stop let me go to the latrine."

"But you can fit just go for here," the man said. "Why wait to go only in a stream?" From the readiness with which he responded, I had the feeling that he had already suspected that the foul odour he smelt was certainly coming from my bowels. Perhaps he thought I had farted or something of the sort.

"I also want to throw some water on my wounds and on my back," I said.

It did not take us long before we reached a stream. Pa Matty rode to the edge of the road and stood, placing his right foot on a stone. I descended and walked tediously down the path that led into the stream. Down the stream I did not go to stool. I took off my clothes, threw away my inner pant, washed the lower part of my body, washed my pair of trousers as best I could, squeezed it and wore it again.

I noticed from the corner of my eye that Pa Matty was watching with infinite patience and curiosity from the road. Although I had been looking for an excuse to clean myself, the water soothed my pains so well that I had no more problem remounting the bicycle. To my conscious self, however, the smell persisted, but grew milder and milder. To completely eradicate the smell I needed to throw away everything I had on and have a hot bath with plenty of soap! That was impossible under the circumstances.

As we rode away the thought of the journey I made a long time ago to Dr. Essemo's house unexpectedly came to my mind. I was in serious pain, but somehow, I thought I felt much more comfortable hanging delicately between two calabashes on the bumping back of the bicycle than I felt in Dr. Essemo's air-conditioned Mercedes!

The tapper rode on, whistling to himself until I asked whether there were other churches around.

"Must be," the man said. "I am not church man," he added. "I only help myself."

"If you are not a church man, and then you do something wrong, how will God forgive you?" I asked. I was anxious that God should know that I was already thinking seriously of Him.

"Why I should I do something wrong?" the man asked. "As I see you and carry you like this, that is wrong?"

I was silent.

"Anyway I was just asking," I said, and inquired where the man was going to when we met.

"I am going to *Diakka,* market. I get my palm trees in Bonkumba. I collect the palm wine and carry to Diakka market. Then after market I buy afofo in this calabash them and return to sell in my place, Komkombunasa. Buy'am sell'am," the man ended up, smiling.

"How many calabashes can you carry on this your Mercedes?" I asked.

"Ten."

"What?"

"Ten," the man said. "You alone, you heavy like six calabash, you no know that?"

I smiled.

"Is morning now," Pa Matty said, pointing to a taxi that had just driven past us.

I did not answer. I had no money on me, so taxi or no taxi, that would make no difference to my fate. At a junction where the man was to branch off we stopped.

"From here you pay 500 francs, they go take you to Azilut Esso. Thas where the AKA church be."

My problems seemed endless. "I have no money, brother," I said. "If you can take me there, I will never forget you. When I see my brother I shall come back to thank you."

"I cannot fit take you there," the man said. "I told you say I am travelling. I have not even tried?"

Coming to look for God, I mused, and yet I was having so much difficulty just to reach the church!

"You have tried," I said. "Only that the thieves took everything." I felt sorry that I was telling all those lies. But since I was going to God, I would be able to explain why I told the lie.

"And me too, no money," Pa Matty complained. "I give you 200 francs and we beg the next taxi," the man suggested.

I took the money, and took the man's address:
Pa Matty
Original White Stuff
(Green Building)
Opposite Fish Point
Swine Quarter, Menako Main Market.

"I will come to thank you some day," I promised. We stopped a taxi. It was Pa Matty who explained to the driver:

He found me man in a gutter, beaten and robbed by thieves. I had been going to see my brother in Azilut Esso. He was going to Diakka market. He had given me 200 francs. The taxi man should take me as far as 200 francs could carry me and leave me.

"If you want help him more than that," Pa Matty added, "God go bless you."

Azilut Esso was 13 kilometres away, but the driver too was a man of understanding and sympathy. He offered to take me right to the church premises.

"There you can get the rest 300 francs from your brother and give me," he suggested.

I agreed, but added:

"His house is a bit far and I do not want to waste your time. Let me take down the number of your car. I will look for you one day and give you the money."

On top of the favour, the taxi man asked me to keep the 200 francs. He wrote his name and address and number of his vehicle on a piece of paper which he gave me.

Chapter Five

Dennis Nunqam Ndendemajem

IT was nearly five o'clock in the morning when the taxi carrying me arrived Azilut Esso. The driver halted in front of a church and asked
"Is this the one?"

It was enough that there was a church, I thought. He looked through the window just for formality and said: "I think it is the place. I have not been there before."

I was in greater pain now that I had been sitting squeezed in the small car. The driver climbed down and walked round to help me get off. The church Pa Matty called Aka was in fact A.L.C.A., an abbreviation for the Angels of Limbo Church of Africa. There was a large signboard by the side of the road to explain it. Slowly I mounted the four steps that led up to the ALCA grounds.

The church building was an oblong sun-dried brick structure the size of an average tennis court. The roof was very high, so designed certainly, to reduce the intensity of heat during the dry seasons. The walls looked freshly painted with whitewash, even in the darkness. The entire compound was surrounded by a hibiscus hedge that stood about ten metres from the building. I discovered belatedly that to the left of the entrance there was a drive way into the premises up which a car, bicycle or motorcycle could drive easily.

Near the gable end to the back a passage led from a door to a smaller attachment. I walked slowly but apprehensively to the back towards the right, came back to the front and walked to the back again towards the left. A bush lamp shone on a rope from the roof of the veranda of the small house.

I was just about to turn back when a voice shouted from a barricaded store to the back of the attachment.

"Who that? You be tifman? Go underwise I shoot!"

"Morning, sir," I greeted politely.

The night watchman emerged from the storeroom, spear in hand and came nearer to where I was standing.

An albino night watchman, I said to himself. I had never seen one.

"Who be you?" the man asked.

"Dennis Nunqam Ndendemajem," I answered.

"You want what?" the albino asked fiercely. This stranger, he was convinced, must be one of numerous drunkards or thieves he chased off every night.

I did not respond at once. I looked round to be sure that we were alone.

"I want to see God," I said rather preposterously.

"He hask you for come for night?" the albino asked. I am sure he now took me for a drunkard.

"Yes," I said.

The man smiled, took out his snuff box and drew in a few nailfuls. He was glad he had company, especially as I did not look dangerous or threatening.

"You say what?" he asked again.

I repeated gravely.

"God or Our Father?" the man inquired.

"Yes," I said dubiously.

Then you must wet unti nan aclock," the albino said.

"What happens at nine?" I inquired

"Our Father comes."

I reflected. We must be talking at cross-purposes, I thought.

"He comes from where?" I asked.

"From **Corony**, na."

It was at this point that I realised that the man was referring not to God himself but to a real person, the man I would be introduced to as the Reverend Pastor Sixtus Shrapnel, the founder of ALCA who lived in a place called **Salvation Colony** at Gemnhenna. He visited his three churches in the Menako region and held services in turns, going to a different one each Sunday.

"Why would they call him Our Father, why would they call him God?" I asked.

"Is his name, is his good work," the man explained. "He make the blind to see, the lame to work, the hungry to have food, the deaf to hear, the dumb to talk," the man recited to me. I say "recited" because he was more fluent when talking about the pastor than when talking about any other subject. I was sure he had been trained to say that about the Pastor. "He is the God of Menako," the man continued. "Between Our Father and God, no difference."

I put my hands over my face and could feel the pain evaporate gradually. I was very close to God, I said to myself. And the ease with which everything had gone was a strong evidence that I had taken the best decision.

Chapter Six

Dennis Nunqam Ndendemajem

At 10 o'clock, one hour later than I had been told, a black Volvo car drove into the ALCA premises. Brother Moses, a church warden to whom the albino night watch had introduced and handed me over, ran up to the car, opened the door and waited. A white man gave a leather brief case to him along with a bundle of keys while still sitting in the car. Brother Moses actually ran to the small house, opened the door with a key and placed the bag on the table and began dusting the room.

The occupant of the car took out a small comb and, looked into his car mirror, ran the comb over his hair several times, picked up a bible and a newspaper and stepped out of the car.

I studied him quickly and carefully. He must have been about fifty years of age or just above. He was tall, broad-chested and very much on the muscular side. He seemed even in his cassock to have a very well-developed upper body that made him look more like a wrestler than a preacher.

He had an aquiline nose, deep penetrating eyes and wore a pair of owl spectacles. I discerned an illusive expression in his face, an admixture of friendliness and hardness. He was wearing a spotlessly white shirt and long green tie over a well ironed charcoal grey pair of trousers.

The pastor took a brief look round the church, greeting the members of his congregation that had started arriving. He seemed to be enormously loved and respected. Everywhere he passed he was greeted with.

"Our Father, good morning."

Having learnt of some of the pastor's activities, and in order to ensure that the pastor received me well, I had found it necessary to tell another lie. I had told Brother Moses that I had been sent from Mbongo to deliver a message personally to the pastor. I was most anxious to talk to him. Thus, no sooner had the pastor entered his office than I urged the warden to announce my presence.

The pastor clenched a thick pencil between his thumb and index finger which he tapped on the bible before him.

"What exactly is your problem, brother?" he asked me in a very charming and friendly manner. "You look so pensive, so apprehensive..."

I looked back out. I was afraid that somebody might be listening.

"You have said it, Pastor," I began very slowly and then I introduced myself to him.

"They call me **Our Father**," he said when I kept calling him Pastor.

"Our Father," I corrected myself and then went on to retell very succinctly the story of what had happened to me down to minute I was talking to him.

Our Father sat back, nodding in silence, his eyes closing and opening as he seemed to rock forth and back.

"In the end," I concluded, "I took a rope and climbed to the roof of the house to hang myself. The roof collapsed. When they rescued me I tried to beg them to forgive me..."

"Who are the **they** here?" he inquired.

"The friend of mine, Dr. Maximillian Essemo Aleukwinchaa and my wife, Manda," I told him."

"I am listening," he said.

"They all refused to forgive me for what I had tried to do. They all said I should go to God, that only God alone can forgive me."

"And so you have come that ALCA should help you gain forgiveness from God?"

I hesitated for a while and then said, "if it is possible, pastor. Our Father, I mean." It was not easy for me to begin calling him **Our Father** like those who had been with him for a long time.

"It is possible," he said. "There is no sin too big to be forgiven, if only you truly repent."

I breathed in and out. Tried in my mind to repeat the words he had just uttered: "There is no sin too big to be forgiven if you truly repent."

"My sin is big, Our Father," I told him, "But I am ready to repent. I am ready to repent."

"I make a wager," Our Father said.

I sat up and looked into his glittering eyes.

"Yes, Father," I said.

"Let us say I lead you to God to listen to you and forgive you as I have done to hundreds of your people, will you carry the cross of Jesus, Brother Dennis?"

"I will carry his anything, Our Father," I promised. "When, how do I start carrying it?"

"You will carry his cross by placing your services at the disposal of the scum of the earth which he has commandeered me to take care of at the **Salvation Colony**."

"The what, Our Father?"

"The scum, people less fortunate than yourself. They are my flock. They live with me in **Salvation Colony** where God gives me the strength to take care of them. Are you ready to do Jesus and me that little favour?"

"I am, Our Father," I accepted.

"E-i-men, brother Dennis," Our Father said. I looked at him as he went on "It is written: Proverbs chapter 28, verse 13. *'He who covers his sins will not prosper, but whoever confesses and forsakes them will have mercy.'* E-i-men."

"Amen," I found myself saying as though the man's words had cast a hypnotic spell on me. In fact if he asked me to do anything right then, I would have done so. He was still talking:

"And that is why Luke Chapter 14 verse 11 says *'whoever exalts himself will be humbled, and he who humbles himself shall be exalted.'* E-i-men."

"Amen," I responded, though I pronounced the words my own way.

He glanced at his watch for the third time, looked out of the window and said:

"Attend this service, and when it is over, come and see me again. I will arrange for you to come to **The Colony**."

"Thank you, Our Father," I said.

***

The church service started at 11 o'clock. At about that hour the pastor put on a coat and tie and walked into the church through the back door at the gable end where the small house was situated. The stage had long been set: a large mahogany table to the right of a rostrum on a dais. On the table was a bottle of mineral water and a glass. On the rostrum was a very large bible.

The middle door through which the pastor came in led into a passage that separated the dais from the rest of the benches on which the congregation sat. When I came in I took my seat in an isolated corner in the front row. That was even because I did not see a chair on which I could sit alone, apart from everybody else. If I had my way I would have preferred to hide in the back row. But I chose the front row because I wanted to be seen. I wanted Our Father to know that I had not disobeyed him just in case he looked round to ensure that I was actually in there as he had asked me to do.

Three things bothered me very much. This first was the fear that God may finally not accept and forgive me for my sins, in spite of the fact that Our Father had given me that assurance. Secondly I knew that I was not clean. Even though I had a hasty rubdown in the stream, I could smell it myself that I was very dirty, and that people sitting by me would soon feel uncomfortable. Many of them were dressed in their best Sunday clothes. Some, though, were dirtier than myself. I saw one whom I thought was a mad man, not a poor man. At first I felt relieved when I noticed him. But when I looked at him again it looked like he was a mad man, not a poor man. And then my worries came back again when I asked myself whether I should be comparing myself with mad people. Was I mad? I was not.

A third reason that kept me uneasy was the fact that I had not been to church for over a decade and so it took me a very long time, in fact all morning, to try and adjust in the new environment. I felt that it would be a shame if somebody noticed from my behaviour that I had not been to church before. I wanted to do what they were doing. And so I spent most of the time looking at others, trying to imitate them.

During the first few minutes I could not resist looking round at the walls too behind the pole. The walls were painted white. Behind the rostrum was a stained glass window with the painting of a lamb holding a banner. Above the stained glass were the words:

The Lord is my Sheppard,
I shall not want.

On the wall to the left where I sat was a painting of Jesus with open hands, looking up towards heaven. Above the painting were the words:

Jesus Saves

On the right wall there was a painting of Jesus blessing little children.

Above the painting were the words:

Suffer little children to come unto me.

There were certainly many other paintings and captions on the walls behind me, but I did not feel comfortable turning right round to look at them all.

Chapter Seven

Dennis Nunqam Ndendemajem

S o much happened that was of very little interest to me. For one thing all of it, the singing and praying sitting and standing, sitting and standing, were entirely new to me. They sat and rose at disorderly intervals. The last church I attended was the catholic mission where I knew when to sit down or stand. In the case of ALCA I felt not only lost but in severe pain. I think the main reason I had problems following was because I had my mind fixed on my own mission, to ask God or to be led to God to ask for forgiveness. Once when the pains in my body were coming back again, I folded my hands and placing my head on them on the back rest of the pew in front of me I dozed off.

When I woke up I had missed a lot. The pastor was on the sermon which he had introduced as **STANDING FOR JESUS**. Pastor Shrapnell was at his best, and it seemed impossible not to like him. His voice and conviction behind it was not only extraordinary but enigmatic. His knowledge of the scriptures and his own personality were overwhelming. His physical appearance from any angle, projected enormous magnetism.

When he spoke everybody nodded, be it the rich or the beggar from the streets. I saw in him and everybody saw no less, that he was nothing else but the pure, devoted man of God sent to save from eternal damnation, those like myself who listened and were ready to follow him.

He quoted extensively from the Bible, but he did not as much as open it throughout the sermon. He would jump down from the dais and virtually touch the listeners to emphasize his point. When he spoke everybody listening seemed to receive the message as though he spoke to him or her directly, personally.

"Let nobody fool you," he was saying when I came back to my senses. "Whether you are blind, deaf, lame, short, or fat, you are the salt of the earth. You are each of you, a spark of the Divine, struck off on the anvil of creation, given life and identity in God the Father, mother of all things, E-i-men," he said.

"E-i-men!" we all responded. This time I pronounced Amen like the others: "E-i-m-e-n."

I stared at him speechlessly, dazed with amazement and admiration. The preacher continued:

"And only you alone must fan this spark through the fire of your own experience, until that day when conscious awareness of the God presence within you is attained.

"Do not ask yourself, 'but why am I like this? Why did God make me so different from other people?' You are an expression of the Godhead. God is infinite and so, man, created in his own image, must be infinite. That multiplicity of differences is a manifestation of the infinite nature of God. So, thank God for making you what you are, E-i-men," he shouted.

The congregation shouted "E-i-men."

"Thank you so very much," he said.

"Standing for Jesus, means sacrifice," Pastor Shrapnell began. "When you have made the choice to follow Jesus, there should be no turning back. For no man having put his hand on the plough and looking back is fit for the kingdom of heaven."

I nodded and looked slightly to my left. Many other persons had joined me in that row. The man sitting next to me was also nodding.

"The life of Saint Francis of Assisi," he said, "is an example which we must emulate, in a world obsessed with money power. The real name of the man we call St Francis of Assissi was Giovanni Bernadone," Pastor Shrapnell said, "the son of a prosperous merchant. Many of us are sons and daughters of the rich. His rich father spoiled him just as we rich parents do. Giovanni lacked nothing and squandered lavishly on friends and women. Who of you will not, who has more than he needs, more than he can ever spend, if he or she is young, handsome, beautiful and rich?

"Once as he rode abroad he was approached by a leper. If there was anything this rich young man could not stand it was a leper. And we can understand that too because throughout the ages leprosy has been the disease of horror.

Giovanni, like all rich men reached for his purse and took out money. Then a light dawned on his heart as it has dawned on many of you sitting here." he pointed individually to the people.

"It was not alms that the poor wretch needed. More terrible than the disease must be the loneliness of the unloved human being." Here he paused and then asked:

"Who has ever felt lonely in a world so full of people?"

I looked round. Some five people put up their hands. I also lifted up mine.

"I mean the kind of loneliness that makes you ask why in this world did God create you. Put down your hands," he said. "When you look the way you do, but feel lonely, blame yourself, because the choice is yours to get back into the human community. One with God is majority.

"But the leper has no chance. He is condemned to a permanent life of loneliness. Leaping from his horse, Francis, rich as he was born and condemned to be, ran to the leper and did what none of you sitting in here will ever do. He embraced and kissed the leper. Not only that, he forced himself to go constantly to the leper hospital. The

35

rich no longer give money to the poor." He shook his head in disappointment. "Send a basket round for alms, and a man who has put in 500 francs, takes away 1000 francs for change."

There was a slight chuckle from the back benches.

"Francis was soon giving all his spending money to help support the hospital and the church of San Damiano. Listen to this one," he smiled to himself. "I wrote a letter out to some businessmen in town here asking for support for the orphanage that I have almost completed single-handedly. Do you know what one of them did?"

He braced himself and said with a smile playing at the corners of his mouth: "The man wrote back:

Dear Pastor Shrapnell;
You are the best thing that has happened to this province since
independence... Let me show you how much I appreciate what you
want to do. I know that an orphanage cannot function without orphans.
So I am sending you here two orphans to show my support.

There was laughter across the hall. I turned round and looked and tried to laugh too but it would not work. Why would I laugh? I had come to look for God, not to laugh. I turned quickly back to look at Pastor Shrapnell.

"Yes, that's how our rich men help the poor," he shook his head again. "One day in 1206, when Francis was 25, he was sent to the town of Foligno to sell merchandise at a fair where he haggled and sold everything, including even the horse he rode to market. On foot he set out for home, unaware that he had transacted the last business deal of his life. For as he walked home through the ripening vineyards a great revulsion against all kinds of money-getting seized him. From possessions, he decided, stemmed all the ugly bickering and soulless grime that dirtied the world. Tell me, how many people in here have ever turned their back on wealth, on luxury?"

I lifted my hand and when I looked back and found that nobody else did, I put it back down.

I noticed that Pastor Shrapnell's eyes turned on me. I was a bit worried because I did not know whether I had offended or impressed him. But the expression on his face was a kind one, not one of condemnation.

"While contemplating these thoughts," he returned to the Francis tale, "he stopped by the chapel of San Damiano and knelt amidst the ruins. Down there in the city, prosperity was god. But God's house here on the peaceful hill was crumbling away. No one tended it but an old priest, poor as the doves settling to roost in the eaves. And it seemed to Francis that he heard Christ's voice saying: 'rebuild my church.' Francis went in, roused up the old priest of the chapel and offered him all the money he had made. I mean ALL the money. He then stripped off the clothes bought with his father's money. Henceforth the world would be his only home, and all men his brothers.

"Never would property fetter his feet. He stripped off his clothes," Pastor Shrapnell said, grabbing the helms of his cassock and lifting them, exposing his well-ironed pair of *tergal* trousers. "How many of you sitting in here have ever, alone, stripped off their clothes, sat down alone in the midst of prosperity, to contemplate God?" he shouted. When he repeated the question, I again lifted my hand and looked round. Again I was the only one. And indeed I had stripped myself naked in Dr. Maximillian Essemo's house. But I had not stripped to contemplate God. I cannot even remember what I was thinking about when Dr. Essemo came into that room and put on the light and insulted me. Once again I was afraid that Pastor Shrapnell would think I was just pretending in order to impress him

"And so Francis set forth in rags to beg not for food or for money - but for stones to rebuild San Damiano. If he was given money he bought stones with it and carried them on his back to the ruined church. And now volunteers joined to help him. When he preached the word of God, he stood not on a pulpit but barefooted in the midst of his fellows, poorer even than they.

"Francis was interested not in the weakness of men but in their strength, not in the ugliness of life but in its beauty. From his overflowing heart burst forth songs of praise.

"Now brethren, what was it that transformed Giovanni Bernadone from the spendthrift lecherous millionaire to a poor servant of the Lord? What converted him from the builder of mansions to the builder of souls?" he asked aloud, perspiration pouring down his forehead.

"It is what has brought you, you, you and you, here today," he stepped down and actually touched individually those of us in the front rows. "It was not thunder, it was a sudden awareness, a flashing illumination in the interior consciousness. This flashing illumination, dear brethren in Christ, is not a plant that grew only in the garden of Francis of Assisi. It is a feeling that converted the love for the world into a repulsion, a feeling that replaced the love of money with an attraction towards God."

There were nods from all corners. I was nodding even before I turned round to look at the others.

"How many of us are ready to turn our backs irrevocably on prosperity, on fame, and work in the name of God to make this world a better place than we met it?"

All hands shot into the air. Pastor Shrapnell nodded with apparent satisfaction and said:

"Thank you. Thank you so very much. E-i—m-e-n."

"E-i-m-en," we all answered.

As I said before, it was the first church service I was attending for over ten years. It was the most momentous sermon I had ever heard, not just because I was looking for God.

"Now, brethren, let us bow our heads and pray to God to give us what we most need," he said solemnly. Then, as I was to discover his comic nature was, he added:

"But don't overwhelm God. What do I mean?" he smiled faintly. The entertainment seemed endless. Even I who for long took a most cynical look at life was beginning to enjoy the humour.

"Once in Ngomgham, down in the valley of the Mezam river, a man sat. It was rainy season and the river had overflowed its banks. Suddenly he saw a television passing in rain water. Having none, he jumped and grabbed it and put on his table, tested it, it worked well. The following day, at two when the rain usually fell heavily, he sat at his veranda again, waiting for a second miracle. Again God took pity on him and he soon saw a video deck sailing down.

"Once again he grabbed it and put on the television. A human being with an appreciative heart would now have gone to the market to buy a cassette to play on the God-given machines. Rather than do this, as soon as rain began falling the next day our friend who would not allow God have a minute's rest, entered the river to catch a passing video cassette. Of course the current swept him away.

"That was a grievous fault. God will not do everything for you. There is so much you can do for yourself."

There was a low long laugh and chuckles from all over. Pastor Shrapnell had not finished tickling us!

"But, again, do not be afraid to tell God your needs, loud and clear," he resumed. "There is this one: Two people were praying. One, a rich transporter was asking God for means to rebuild the engine of his Mercedes truck, something like 5 million francs. And the other, a poor man was asking aloud that God should give him another chain for his motorcycle. The rich man seemed to take offence that the poor man was making it hard for God to listen to him.

39

"What do you want?" the rich man asked.

The poor man explained: "Only a chain and you will not allow God to hear me? How much money?" the rich man asked.

The poor man told him.

"Only 3,000 francs, and you will not allow God to hear me? Take this and go away so that God can listen to more important things."

"He gave the poor man 5,000 francs.

When the man got home he told his wife he came to church, prayed and God gave him 5000 francs for his chain!"

He too smiled, causing the congregation to burst into laughter once more.

"Brethren, let us now talk to God, each in his own way," he said sombrely.

I wondered how many people were looking at me and asking themselves why I was behaving like somebody who had never been to church before. I was careful to do just what the others were doing. "Forgive me, God. I have offended everybody, I have come to ask Our Father to lead me to you to ask for pardon," I said and looked up.

Chapter Eight

Dennis Nunqam Ndendemajem

I was the subject of the last part of the service.

The Pastor said: "As we bow down our heads to communicate with God, I take this very special opportunity to show here our newest brother. Brother Dennis, stand up," he beckoned to me.

I rose.

"Introduce yourself and tell the church why you are here."

"I am Dennis Nunqam Ndendemajem. I was working with the Central Cooperatives in Mbongo. Because of my lowly position a friend of mine came and took me to live with him and study to become a doctor. Life became so complicated that I took a rope and climbed to hang myself..."

There was a low noise of disapproval.

"Yes, brethren," Pastor Shrapnell stepped in. "Give him your ears."

"The roof fell on me. I felt sorry and went to everybody who knew me to ask for forgiveness. They all refused. So I have come to Our Father," I pointed to Pastor Shrapnell, the man nodded.

"He has agreed to talk to God on my behalf and God will listen to me, and He will forgive me. And I have pledged my services at the disposal of Salvation Colony, forever."

"E-i-men, Brethren!" Pastor Shrapnell shouted from the pulpit and clapped.

"E-i-m-e-nnn!" they all shouted and clapped.

"Resume your seat, brother Dennis," he said.

I felt some slight relief, not from the pain in my body but in the pain in my heart, the pain on my mind. Even without actually talking to God I began to feel wanted. As I sat down Pastor Shrapnell concluded:

"Even as we are rejoicing here, brethren, there is joy in heaven for our brother. For Luke Chapter 15 verse 7 tells you that *there is more joy in heaven over one sinner who repents than over 99 respectable people who do not need to repent.*"

***

As soon as the service was over I waited for The Pastor at the door of his office. When he came he placed his right hand on my shoulder and took me into the office. There he asked me to confirm that I had once actually turned my back on wealth, and that I had once actually taken off my clothes and sat alone to contemplate the greatness of God.

"Dr. Maximillian Essemo is wealth," I said. "I turned my back on his wealth. In his own house I lived only in the boys' quarters, not in the luxurious main house. One day I removed all my clothes and sat in the dark. But, Our Father," I confessed, "when I removed my clothes and sat in the dark it was not because I was thinking of God. I was just thinking of my misery in a world where everybody else was enjoying himself.

The Pastor seemed doubly pleased with me.

"I see in your eyes that the Lord has already pardoned you all your sins," he said. I don't know whether he meant to be taken seriously, but the more he reassured me the better I felt both in my heart and in my body.

"What makes you think so, Pastor?" I asked.

"I have spoken to Him in my heart," he said, "and he has assured me that he has done so, if you will carry his cross."

"I will carry it, Pastor," I promised again. "Just show me and I will carry it."

"Come to the Colony," the Pastor repeated the invitation.

"I am in pain, Our Father," I told him. "I am hungry, I have nothing, no food, no money. What you see on me is all that I have on this earth as clothes. I am not even wearing a pant inside."

"Come to Salvation Colony," Pastor Shrapnell said again. "At Salvation Colony, the Lord ensures that those who do not have, have. You will lack nothing." Pastor Shrapnell gave me 2,000 francs and told me to find my way to Salvation Colony. "You can't miss it," he said and then drove away.

Chapter Nine

Dennis Nunqam Ndendemajem

S alvation Colony or simply **The Colony**, was indeed
a place one could not easily miss. It was located at
27 kilometres from the church where I had met
Pastor Shrapnell. A large marble block of about two meters
square stood on the left side of the road as you drove down.
On both sides it bore the information:

SALVATION COLONY
OF THE ANGELS OF LIMBO CHURCH OF AFRICA
A SPECIAL GIFT
FROM THE A.C.C.A

The colony itself was completely walled in barbed wire
and cypress so well protected that it was not easy to go in
through any other means than the main entrance. The
entrance itself was about five meters wide, with a large iron
gate. There was evidence of Godliness or of the scriptures
all over the place. Above the gate and carved in bold lettering
on a cement arch spanning the width of the gate was the
message which Pastor Shrapnell had dealt out to me that
morning:

NO SIN IS TOO BIG TO BE FORGIVEN,
IF ONLY YOU TRULY REPENT

Each of the two pillars carrying the iron gate bore a
religious message. The pillar on the right said:

JESUS HEALS. Under the message was a wooden carving of a black Jesus placing his hand on a sick man with others looking on. The pillar on the left read:
CHRIST CARRIED YOUR CROSS,
WHY NOT CARRY YOUR BROTHER'S?
Below that too, was the carving of Jesus carrying a cross.

You passed through a thick canopy of sweet-smelling flowers over an archway that was about ten meters long, ending in a smaller door that led into a large waiting area. To the left of the inner door was a large garage. There were several benches of the sort you find in front of consultation rooms in hospitals. To the right of the waiting area was a library and reading room. Over the door there was the inscription:

THE GLORY OF THE WORLD WOULD
BE BURIED IN OBLIVION HAD NOT GOD
AS A REMEDY CONFERRED ON MAN
THE BENEFIT OF BOOKS

The floor which was carefully cemented was painted red and looked very clean. The benches seemed concentrated mainly to the left as you entered the gate. On the wall above the benches to the left was a quotation from Lowell, which read:

THE WORLD IS PURIFIED NOT BY ACTION,
BUT BY NOBLENESS OF LIFE.
THEREFORE, BE NOBLE AND THE
NOBLENESS THAT LIES IN OTHER MEN,
SLEEPING BUT NEVER DEAD WILL RISE IN
MAJESTY TO MEET THINE OWN.

On the opposite wall at almost the same level was another quotation, this time from Seneca. It read:

LIVE AMONG MEN AS IF GOD BEHELD YOU; SPEAK TO GOD AS IF MEN WERE LISTENING

There was a large polished wooden door in the middle of the wall to the extreme left side with a small table near the door. There was a tall, lean gentleman with thin hands and a thin neck sitting at a desk. He received me and chatted with me and kept me company while I waited to see the Pastor. An albino sat at another table nearest the door into the Pastor's office. Above the door was a religious message:

HOW LOVELY IS YOUR DWELLING PLACE (Ps.83)

HOW GREAT IS YOUR NAME, O LORD (Ps.8)

Near the door nub there was another message:

KNOCK AND IT SHALL BE OPENED
UNTO YOU (Matt.7.7)

That was Pastor Shrapnell's office. I would discover later that there was a door in the office that opened into his bedroom which was a few steps lower than the level of the office and waiting area. Thus he could move from his bedroom to his office and back without being seen. His kitchen and bathroom were attached to his bedroom, with a small door opening into a garden at the back of the house.

The ladies' hall of residence was about 10 meters away with a toilet separating it from Shrapnell's block. On the pink wall was a message in large black letters:

YOU GIVE BUT LITTLE IF YOU OF YOUR
POSSESSIONS GIVE.
IT IS WHEN YOU GIVE OF YOURSELF THAT
YOU TRULY GIVE.
(Khalil Jebran)

A large playground spanned the area between the gable end of the ladies' building and the southern corner of the main fence.

Partly facing the ladies' hall about 50 meters away was a vestibule about 25 meters in length and 20 in width. They called it WISDOM HALL. On the door was the inscription:

TO GET GOOD IS HUMAN
TO DO GOOD IS HUMAN
TO BE GOOD IS DIVINE

It was the main prayer hall. It had something like a stage which could also serve as a pulpit. There were over 300 chairs and a handful of benches along the walls. Directly behind WISDOM HALL was a slightly smaller hall. It was the dining hall. On the walls of each of the walls was a religious message or a painting of some religious figure or event.

To the back of the dining hall and almost spanning **WISDOM HALL,** was one of three halls of residence for men. The buildings were interspersed with flower beds and gardens. Behind the men's buildings were farms and two buildings which served as handicraft centres. On each side of the walls between which the road led to the farms and the handicraft centre, were carved the words:

LABORARE EST ORARE

Over the door of the handicraft centre was a quotation from Horace:

FOR A WEB BEGUN, GOD SENDS THREAD

There were two drinking wells to supplement the tap water, a private generator to supplement the electricity from the National Electric Corporation. There was a corn mill, a small poultry farm and a piggery overlooking a large fishpond. **Salvation Colony** as I discovered that same day, was virtually a world, complete in itself.

The Colony had a small post office and an infirmary, a bookshop that sold mainly religious literature, a canteen and a recording office that sold cassettes of songs by the various choirs. **Salvation Colony** also owned a twelve seater bus which it used mainly for its Gospel Crusades.

Pastor Shrapnell himself, Our Father, drove a Volvo 504. It was so well-furnished within, it was usually said, that it lacked only a toilet. Somebody said to me that it had "an automatic toilet" inside. Whether it meant that he could drain his bowels without making a move, I could not tell because I heard that he always drove the car alone.

Chapter Ten

Dennis Nunqam Ndendemajem

W hen did you last go to church?" Pastor Shrapnell asked me when it was finally my turn and I entered his office to talk to him.

"About ten years ago," I said in my throat and then lifted my head and looked into his face, expecting the worse.

I noticed that he did not look as alarmed or disturbed as I was fearing he would.

"That's pretty long," he said, shaking his head more in obvious sympathy than condemnation.

"That is the precise beginning of the problem you have," he said. "You had abandoned God."

A very long silence followed and then I, bent on defending myself said:

"Sir, but I know of people who have not been to church for 20 years, and they are happy...."

"That is true, brother Dennis," he said. "Sin and suffering are two different things. Being in a state of sin is not like being in a state of epidemic or plague where all affected persons must die, as soon as they catch it. Some of those you think are happy are **not** actually. There are many, very many who are doomed. They, unlike you, are irretrievable."

I looked at him in surprise.

"Oh yes," the man nodded. "Those individuals don't have to. They do the will of God. When a man suddenly becomes conscious of sin as you have done, it is an indication that he does not belong to the world of sin. It shows he can be saved as you are about to do."

51

"You mean I can be saved, sir? I mean, Pastor, Our Father?" I asked. One moment I would believe that I would be saved, the other moment I would think that I could not be saved.

"I don't see why not," he said. "At the gate the message is clear:

THERE IS NO SIN TOO BIG TO BE
FORGIVEN
IF ONLY YOU ARE TRULY SORRY.

"My wife, my friends, my relatives, they may never forgive me," I said almost to myself.

"They don't have to," Shrapnell said. "God's forgiveness is all that matters. In John chapter 15 verses 18 and 19, Jesus tells his disciples: *If the world hates you, just remember that it has hated me first. If you belonged to the world, then the world would love you as its own. But I chose you from this world, and you do not belong to it; that is why the world hates you.*

"Next week is Soul to Soul," he continued, "you will find that you have done very little to be worried about. As I said in church, I will personally present your case to God and ask Him to forgive you, and my heart tells me that He will forgive you your sins."

"For how long are you here? For how long do you want to carry the cross of Jesus?"

"For as long as you are here, Our Father. Nobody wants me. If you want me, I shall be here forever."

"You are my child," he said with profound tenderness which almost moved me to tears. "Everybody here is my child. Christ said it all in Matthew 19, verse 13: *'suffer little children to come unto me. Forbid them not, for of such is the kingdom of heaven...*E-i-m-e-n."

"E-i-m-e-n," I replied.

"First thing, you must find your feet in this colony," he said. "To help anybody you must be able to stand on your own feet. What do you do best?"

I rubbed my hands together, grimaced, rubbed my eyes with the back of my right hand and remained silent. The last time that question was thrown at me was when Dr. Essemo had come for me and we were travelling back to his house, my hell. When I told him to choose what he would like to have me do, he had suggested the impossible, that I should do medicine, that I should be a doctor, that medicine was the profession of professions!

I had come to look for God. I would not give an answer which would make me lose that chance. Pastor Shrapnell had some mysterious power of reading people's minds. He immediately saw that I was confused.

"Just tell me what kind of thing you can do so that we help you realise that here," he explained. "You will not spend all the waking hours in prayer. God may soon get bored with your prayers," he ended up with a smile.

I still did not answer.

"Can you drive a vehicle?" he asked.

"No, Our Father," I said.

"Can you make a carving?" he asked and then went on to other questions even before I answered.

"Repair radios, motor cars, type documents, build houses, and the like?"

I shook my head in denial.

"Can you sew clothes?"

"I can patch clothes."

"I mean cutting and stitching them..."

"I cannot."

"Blacksmith?"

"No."

He made as if he was searching his mind for a solution. Then he finally settled on art.

"Can you draw and paint?" he asked.

I did not shake my head in denial. I stared at him. It was evident that I was not quite sure whether I was good enough to admit that I could draw and paint. Again, the mind-reading Pastor read my thoughts instantly.

"Can you draw?" the man repeated.

"I can try," I said timidly.

Shrapnell pulled out a piece of paper from his drawer, picked up a pencil from the desk before him and tossed it to me. "Draw a thief," he said.

I took the paper and pencil, adjusted the pencil on the paper and then asked the man: "You say I should draw who?"

"A thief."

Something happened to my whole body. Down the pit of my stomach I felt the muscles contract, such as I could scarcely recall ever having undergone. I felt a sudden compression of my chest or was it my lungs? It was as if I was standing before an X-ray machine, as if I was taking in a long deep breath and wanted to breathe out.

Pastor was looking at me. I sensed the upper side of my mouth and its corners draw apart and upward. I sensed my eyelids rising on their own, and my nostrils opening and closing. There was a vibration in my lower jaw. At the same time my eyes began to water and the vibration in my jaw moved to my chest which ended with a mild explosion of laughter.

I found myself laughing. Me, laughed! I immediately pulled myself together and then said: "I am sorry, Our Father. I did not mean to laugh at you."

"Why sorry?" he asked, looking straight into my eyes. "I laugh a lot myself. Laughter, they say, is the best medicine."

It was the first time I had actually laughed from the heart in about ten years. My eyes were still watering when I asked: "How, sir, would a thief look?"

"Like a thief," he said comically. Both of us laughed again and then the Pastor said: "Draw your right hand or a hand holding an umbrella, or something of the sort. Anything."

After that laugh, I felt reborn in me a sudden relief. It was as though I had taken a purgative, for the laugh seemed to have sucked from the bottom of my stomach all the cares of this life that had burdened me for years. I suddenly saw myself thinking unimpeded.

The result of this transformation was that I drew both the hand and umbrella with the curved handle of the umbrella resting on a left hand that lay on the table.

Pastor Shrapnell was very impressed with the speed and effortless manner with which the exercise was executed. I felt very happy with myself that I had impressed him. Out of the sheer joy of doing it, I proceeded to shade the drawing, even after Pastor Shrapnell was satisfied with the overall performance.

"You have a jewel right there in your palms," he said to me.

I felt flattered. I smiled, there was a tinge of uncertainty in it.

"Seriously," Pastor Shrapnell said.

"How far can one go with art, Our Father," I inquired, "when there are such professions as medicine and engineering?"

It was as if I had opened the tap from which nothing but art could flow. "Art will take you anywhere," he began. "It will take you to the furthest point on this planet. It will take you to heaven. Forget about doctors and engineers. A doctor or an engineer is only better than an artist if he can be an artist in addition to being a doctor or an engineer. How many of doctors and engineers lived during the lifetime of Leonardo da Vinci, of Michelangelo, of Rembrandt, of Picasso? Hundreds. And yet how many are remembered today like these artists?"

I sat silent. There was no stopping him.

"The *Summa Artis - Historia General del Arte* defines man as "an animal that has an aesthetic capacity," he said. "A knowledge of art such as you have displayed, and such as I can guess you are capable of achieving, I bet you, establishes a direct link between you and God. If you came here looking for God, you have found him. In your own very self."

He reached for the Bible from his shelf, opened to Genesis 1.27 and asked me to read. I took the book and read out softly:

"... *God proceeded to create the man in his image, in God's image he created him.*"

"The Bible is not saying that our first parents looked like God," he added wryly. "Rather, God endowed them with attributes he himself possessed. One of these is the ability to appreciate beauty. To know art is to know beauty, which is next to knowing God. To love art is to love God who is, by the way, the first and greatest artist, the artist behind all artists. "Have you ever taken time to see a glorious sunset, the colours of a peacock, the iridescent scales on the wings of a butterfly, the rose flower, a waterfall, a desert sand dune, the geometric intricacy of a spider's web?"

"I do, once in a while," I admitted.

"You do?"

"I do."

"And you need to be convinced further that God is a lover of beauty, that he is an artist? The line between art and divinity is a straight one. All that artists are doing on this earth is copying nature. Michelangelo once said '*the true work of art is but a shadow of the divine perfection.*' In Matthew 6. 28-29, Jesus told his disciples: *take a lesson from the lilies of the field, how they are growing; they do not toil, nor do they spin; but I say to you that not even Solomon in all his glory was arrayed as one of these.*'

"Sir Thomas Browne a seventeenth century physician once said '*Nature is the art of God.*' *And he was very right....*" He paused briefly and then declared: "But you do not even need to go into the fields to admire the artistic miracles of God. A supreme example is your own body. The sculptors of ancient Greece looked on the human form as the epitome of artistic excellence. They therefore strove to represent it as perfectly as is humanly possible. A classic example is the famous painting of Mona Lisa by Leonardo da Vinci. In sculpture we remember the famous statue of David by Michelangelo."

"I think I will continue with my art," I resolved with total conviction. For the first time I had met somebody who loved what I loved and who knew more about what I loved than myself.

"You better," Pastor Shrapnell said. Without knowing that he had completely won me over to art he pointed to a picture of Christ on the wall which he brought down and set on a shelf a little distance away from where we sat. I went closer and looked at the name of the artist.

"That is by Peter Rubens," he cut in. **CHRIST ON THE CROSS** was the title of the painting. He pointed to the dead Christ hanging there alone in the night with drooped head and flowing hair and the background a black sky over the distant Jerusalem. He drew attention to the absence of colour, even though colour was a great feature of Rubens' art.

"**CHRIST ON THE CROSS**," he repeated. "The original hangs in the Old Pinacothek in Munich," "This particular painting may not compare with some of Rubens' other paintings. But see the blinding horror of the scene, the blackness of darkness, the awfulness of the deed. The power, the dread, the strength of death are overwhelming. Do you not feel the conviction rushing irresistibly upon you that the crucified hanging upon the cross is not a human being, but the real son of God?"

I looked from the painting to the pastor, baffled by the man's interpretation of art.

"How the mind of Rubens ever soared so high as to grasp that conception baffles comprehension," he went on. "Yet it did, through art. No writer of the Bible could have captured the scene quite the same or even close, in words. Yes, a picture is worth a thousand words, they say."

I walked back and sat down, hushed. I looked at Shrapnell, smiled again and shook my head in admiration.

"I think I will continue with my art," I said once more. I felt born in me an unprecedented consciousness of a supreme power such as I had never felt before. When Dr. Essemo spoke to me it was as though I had engulfed myself with an envelope, a shield through which nothing penetrated, however well-intentioned. With this consciousness of God which I could not now distinguish from supreme art, my mind suddenly became receptive to advice. An inner peace and security had suddenly taken possession of my heart.

Like a patient in agony who had just received a pain-killer, I could feel the gradual disappearance not only of the physical pains, but more importantly, of that perennial tension, the suspicions, the doubts, the weariness and fretting which had stalked my waking hours for the last decade and a half. With the disappearance of this worriness came also a sudden feeling of guilt. Why had I waited for so long to think of God, I wondered.

"How is this your church different from other churches?" I asked after a while.

"You mean churches such as…?"

"The Catholic church, the Apostolic Church, the True Church of God, the Presbyterian Church, Jehovah Witnesses, Deeper life…"

"It is like all those churches," Pastor Shrapnell began, "in that it leads you to God. But it is different from all others in that we do what they do not and cannot do. For instance we live together in one brotherhood, in a colony where the blind, the lame, the deaf, the dumb, the good, the bad, the ugly, are all shown the way to God. It is deeper than Deeper Life, truer than the so-called True Church, witnesses more miracles than the Jehovah Witnesses, preach more gospels than the so-called Full Gospel...."

I was won over, forever. And that was the way Pastor Shrapnell won over his converts. To the blind he cited the cases of Helen Keller, of John Milton the poet, of the musicians Ray Charles and Stevy Wonder and of the Jamaican professor, Wilfred Cartey who supervised doctoral dissertations for scholars like Kofi Awoonor, who had all their eyes intact.

***

There grew between myself and Pastor Shrapnell a bond of friendship and respect that was never to grow between him and any other member of his flock.

Pastor Shrapnell himself said of me that I was the most mentally stable of all his followers, the most generally gifted, the one who could analyse things in detail objectively and maturely, the one who least needed constant attention. He once described me as his most valuable asset.

I discovered that he desperately needed somebody with a practical knowledge of art to decorate **The Colony** and to produce numerous paintings of African scenes which he would send from time to time to his sponsors back in America to show how well he was helping people like us. I told him that I was not only glad to be of use to him, but ready to spend all my time making paintings for his church and for his company back in America.

Chapter Eleven

Dennis Nunqam Ndendemajem

After my consultation with Pastor Shrapnell, and at the end of which I pledged my entire life to the service of **The Colony**, I was led by the pastor himself to one of the male blocks. There were nine people in the hall, each occupying a small cubicle that looked like the private ward in a hospital. In it was a medium-sized **Vono** bed, a foam mattress, a pillow and two bedspreads. There was also a small cupboard, a flask and two Bibles - **GOOD NEWS NEW TESTAMENT** and **THE HOLY BIBLE**.

Two gentlemen came to see me immediately after Pastor Shrapnell left.

"We are the Brethren's Keepers," one said. "I am Brother Walters," he said and then introduced his companion: "This is Brother Ernest." He smiled. "And you, Brother," he looked at me expectantly. I did not hesitate to introduce myself. "I am Dennis Nunqam Ndendemajem," he said. The two brothers looked and behaved in a most friendly and simple manner.

"Praise the Lord," Brother Walters said. "Anything you want to know about this place, ask us. Anything you need, ask us, and we shall ask Our Father, and he will make sure that you have it."

I thanked them.

"Have you eaten, Brother?" one asked.

"Not yet, Brothers," I answered. "Brothers I have just come. I am not very well. There are pains all over my body. I had an injury."

"I will ask them to get you some warm water and some balm," one said.

I felt elated.

"After that, there will be prayers in the chapel, and then supper in the dining hall," Brother Walters said. "I am across," he pointed through the window. "Anything you need, come and tell me. Anything."

As they continued on what looked like their rounds, I drew Brother Walters aside and said:

"Brother, let me tell you at once. I have had so many problems that I just managed to bring only my life here. I will bother you for every single thing. I have no other article of clothing than what you see on me."

"It is understood, Brother Dennis. Your needs will be taken care of. Only trust in God."

"I trust," I said. And, in fact I trusted in God more than they could have believed.

***

As soon as the Brethren left, I was visited by four members of my hall who were somewhere outside in the Colony when I came in. First to come was an albino whom I at first thought was the same person I had met early that morning. He introduced himself as **"Bonblanc."** He was holding the hand of a rather tall gentleman who introduced himself as Brother Tobias Teumick. It would take me one full week to know that Brother Toby who led all discussions and threw jibes at every single person was blind. The third person came in crawling on his buttocks because he was lame. The fourth was a one-eyed dwarf.

For a while the peculiar nature of the people around him stunned me. But I quickly recalled the pastor's words that he had set up The Colony mainly for those on whom society had turned its back. I did not have a watch, and so when I was shown the chapel and told that prayers would be in about an hour, I just walked to the hall and took a seat at the back.

That early departure to church kept the four Keepers very worried, especially when Pastor Shrapnell told them where to place me so that he could introduce me to the others. It was with great relief on their part that they found me sitting at the back of the chapel, gazing at the paintings and writings on the walls.

***

By six o'clock we were all assembled. The women sat mostly to the right because the right middle door faced their halls of residence. There were no fewer than seventy people in the chapel which looked like it could conveniently take a hundred more. Prayers were led by one of the Brethren and that lasted for thirty minutes. Towards the end of the prayer session, Pastor Shrapnell appeared through a door that opened to the back of the pulpit.

"Alleluia," he shouted.

"Praise the Lord," they shouted back.

He looked at Brother Walters, and the latter walked up to me and stood by my side.

"Tiny drops of water…" he began

"Make a mighty ocean," they all answered back.

"Our numbers grow every day. Every day the Lord adds a new leaf and a new branch to this tree which we have planted. Alleluia,"

"Praise the Lord."

"Brother Dennis," he beckoned to me, and when I had come he held up my hand and said: "The Lord added him to us this morning. Whatever he has been in the past, he has thrown away, in order to embrace the future which is the light. E-i-men!" he shouted

63

"E-i-men!" they answered.

"Brother Dennis has come to ask for forgiveness from God for his sins, and in return he will carry the Cross of Jesus by adding the beauty of art to the walls of this church, and to the walls of our hearts. Alleluia!"

"Praise the Lord."

I smiled contentedly and nodded.

"Promise, Brother Dennis."

"I promise," I said.

***

After prayers we went for supper. There were huge pots of corn-chaff, rice and bread. There was no meat, only dried fish. I had more than enough to eat. While I was still at table, a lady came up to me and introduced herself as Sister Rebecca. She was one of the Keepers. She asked me to make two lists, one for the things I would need for the night and one for the things I would need for the week.

I made the two lists without the kind of apprehension which infested my mind whenever Dr. Essemo asked to do anything for me. After supper we broke up into smaller choir groups. Singing lasted for an hour, we prayed for another hour and then retired to our beds for the night.

Chapter Twelve

Dennis Nunqam Ndendemajem

The following day began with prayers, compound care, breakfast and then Human Investment. During the Human Investment period occupants of the Colony broke up again into business groups, or groups of common interest: gardening, carpentry, wood carving, basket weaving, music, drawing and painting. I spent that first morning going from one group to the other, studying them to see into which one I could easily and conveniently fit. Members were permitted and even encouraged to belong to as many groups as possible.

We had lunch at noon, rested for two hours and then broke up into human investment groups. We went for prayers at six, had supper at seven and then broke up into choir groups. The same activities were repeated each day.

Before I went to bed that first night I was given a tooth brush and tooth paste, a tablet of soap, a pair of rubber slippers and a towel. The following day I was given 10,000 francs to do my purchases from the Colony Canteen whence I bought two pants and a few other items.

I was especially amazed by the degree of tolerance exhibited by members of The Colony, most of whom were physically deformed. They all called each other by outrageous nicknames. The totally blind man was called "blackboard." If there were two or three of them, they were called "blackboard 1, or blackboard 2, depending on the order of arrival. The same applied to residents with other disabilities. The lame man was called "Crab," the one-eyed man "cyclops," the albino "redcross," "bonblanc," or "mbobong"; the divorced woman, "ex-service," the barren woman "roadblock." The dwarf was called "inches," and the fingerless lepers "fingerprint."

Each called the other and very cheerfully received these names in return with a smile. One of Shrapnell's writings on the wall of the dining hall read:

**IT IS NOT MISERABLE TO BE BLIND,
OR LAME OR UGLY.
IT IS MISERABLE NOT TO BE ABLE TO
ENDURE
BLINDNESS, LAMENESS OR UGLINESS.**

Inhabitants of The Colony found this a very useful philosophy.

The main problem was with the deaf and dumb. There were some very sad cases: a certain woman was deaf, dumb and blind. There was also a male cripple who had lost his hands and an eye in a motor accident. And there was the very intriguing though pathetic case of Mammy Nyanga, a certain woman whom they also called "bundle". She was born without any limbs. She was not up to a metre in height and her hands from birth, were only two fingerless stumps that terminated at the elbow joints.

Nobody ever knew what her under parts looked like because she always wore a gown that dragged on the floor as she hopped by. She could do just about anything with the stumps. For instance she could take snuff, serve a drink and even write with a pen. She was always the centre of attraction whenever they went out on a crusade.

Probably not more than forty, she had a very beautiful voice and was the leader of one of the choir groups. She was the first to poke fun at her disability. She would tell the others that she was ready to enter heaven because she had made the necessary sacrifice, for it is said that if any part of your body offends you, cut it off. It is better to enter heaven without that part than go to hell with all parts intact. Her pet expression was "I swear by all my limbs that what I am saying is true." One of the startling revelations was made when at a SOUL TO SOUL she said she had once mothered two children both of whom had died in infancy.

***

I checked in on Sunday evening, ailing. By Thursday I was already feeling relieved, thanks to the drugs administered by a resident nurse. I called on Pastor Shrapnell everyday to inquire more and more about The Colony. I felt more comfortable asking Pastor Shrapnell himself than the Keepers. On Friday morning Pastor Shrapnell informed me that we would be having a **SOUL TO SOUL** that evening. He told me what that meant: five members of the Colony would be called upon, each in his own turn, to tell the stories of their misadventures, the events that led him or her to abandon the world outside and take up residence in The Colony.

If an individual had had a problem with anybody, if his or her suffering had been caused by anybody, he described the situation as vividly and as honestly as possible. He was then called upon to forgive the offender. And if, as it sometimes happened, the offender had also found his way into Salvation Colony, the two were caused to stand, declare each other forgiven, embrace and then live happily thereafter as friends.

***

The event took place in the assembly hall immediately after supper. I was sitting near "blackboard", the blind man from my hall, a man who in spite of his handicap had a word for everybody and for everything that was said.

A few spaces from me sat Brother Inches, the dwarf. If you saw only a passport picture of him you would think he was two metres tall. But he was just a little over a metre in height. Again, if you heard him talk you would think it was a child of about eight years talking. But he was about forty-three years old.

He was called Inches not just because he was short but because of an additional infirmity: he had been afflicted by a spinal rupture resulting in what the doctors described as multiple sclerosis. Because of a fracture he moved only a few inches at a time, as if his two legs were tied close to each other with a string.

He played the accordion very well and had once been part of the touring team of a tobacco advertising company. Those days he was the laughing-stock of young women who gave him the impression that he was much loved and that they were all at his beck and call. But he realised after several years that his physique created curiosity not love, and that the public was out simply to ridicule his diminutive structure.

Once, a woman invited him to her room and undressed and stood up in front of him naked. He reached just about her knees. She played with him as if he was a toy, and then dressed up and abandoned him. He felt so bad that he turned his back on women. Soon after that he joined A.L.C.A.

Next to Brother Inches sat "Brother Water Melon," a man afflicted by elephantiasis of the scrotum. Mbobong Paul the albino was the first to speak, it was an exercise he had taken part in several times before.

"Black man white man," the blind man quipped from behind me. Apparently Mbobong knew who had spoken.

"It is even better that I am what I am," Mbobong said with a smile, and in the same spirit of entertainment. "Even if I was black, will you know?" he asked the blind man.

"Arata die," **Blackboard** said.

"Na yi mop," the rest answered.

"Go befo," **Blackboard** said.

"So this is me," Mbobong began again. "People are paying money to go to the white man's country to see white men. My mother delivers me and immediately nobody wants to see me. I was to be the chop chair, but they said an albino could not be the head of the family. My mother gave me medicine to put in the food of the two boys from my step-mothers. They died. Their blood went into my head, the other women and my father knew that my mother and me had killed their children. They chased us away from the family. My mother died soon afterwards. I went from place to place and wherever I went the story was there before me. Nobody wanted to see me. Then I met Our Father into whose hands I threw myself. Now I have found another fellowship in Jesus..."

"And now, Brother Paul," Shrapnell called, "what would you do that you may live in perfect peace and tranquillity in the kingdom of the Lord?"

"Forgiveness. I beg all those whom I have hurt to pardon me. I beg those my two mothers and my father whose two children I poisoned to forgive me. I forgive all those who have in any way hurt me."

"E-i-men!" Shrapnell shouted.

"E-i-men!" they all answered.

"Alleluia!"

"Praise the Lord," we responded. I overheard Blackboard say "Place de hot!"

Chapter Thirteen

Dennis Nunqam Ndendemajem

Next on the podium was Dr. Nigonle Nchutebong alias "Doctor Parrot." He was probably in his mid-sixties with a small head on which his hair grew scantily. His pair of rather small eyes glittered mischievously in their sockets below raised brows. His nose and mouth were small and he always ensured that there was never a strand of hair on his wrinkled face. There were many who had wished that the man had been born without a mouth at all, because of the amount of evil that always came out each time he opened his mouth.

His neck was thin and long and he always wore a scarf as though he was concealing a vicious scar. His arms were very thin with his elbows protruding as though he had a small boil at each tip. His back arched a little probably from age, and he stooped a little as he walked. His buttocks were very flat, accentuating the thinness of his body, since his belly rose in a small mound below his navel.

He was always very neatly dressed and walked as though he was never in a hurry to go anywhere.

"Those who know me well," he began his soul-destroying confession, "know that I was the very first Medical Engineer that this country ever had. A medical Engineer, for those who do not know, is one who repairs hospital equipment - microscopes, X-ray machines, and the like.

"I was also the last because after me, the post was occupied mainly by expatriates. I did much wrong to this country and to my friends as Medical Engineer. I single-handedly killed the General Hospital, particularly the X-ray division. They say if you want to know a man, give him power! The Government gave me power. I set up a private consultancy and a workshop in Alè-ajick behind the Airlines office where I repaired instruments for private hospitals and clinics.

I sent people to disable laboratory equipment which were then brought to my service in town for repairs. I raised pay vouchers of up to 100,000 francs each week on small repairs. Then this was what made me a sinner: once my agents dismantled the X-ray machines during a tuberculosis epidemic and I discovered that I could not fix it as early as I had estimated. Sixty people died because their cases could not be diagnosed."

He smiled to himself as the stunned listeners murmured. Even though they had heard this story many times before, they could not conceal their discomfort.

"That's all behind me," he said.

"And what do you ask of the families you hurt by listening to the voice of the devil, Brother Nchutebong?" Shrapnell asked from his seat.

"Forgiveness," he responded. "And then there is the second case," he continued. "Because of the nature of my education, because of the fact that I had been a sportsman, and because of my profession which brought me into contact with very many people in my life time, the government enticed me into working for them. As multi-partysm was spreading across the continent, the government felt threatened and was anxious to nip every sign of opposition in the bud. I was to be informant, supplying secret information on the activities of suspected persons. The government lived in constant fear of plots to overthrow the President. I was paid enormous sums of money every month for doing nothing, or for doing what I liked to do. I paid no more attention to my engineering profession, which was why they began to call me *"enginieur de conception!*

"The best people I could work with to get at traitors was women, young girls. I never hated a beautiful face in my young years, and had been four times married. As is in the sinful nature of mortal man, I abused the office. Because I had so much money to play with, I wanted all the beautiful women I saw. If a young lady showed any reluctance to accept my request I immediately linked her up with some conspiracy and she suffered accordingly. If she was prevented from falling in love with me because of anybody, I put the man out of my way. I lived on the blood of innocent people. I caused the suffering and death of many persons. There was, in particular, the case of Dr. Bukusi Fanabo who clashed with me over a young lady and would not give up. I framed a case against him that he was planning to form a political party. I worsened the mater by sending a picture of the president with the eyes scratched, to his chamber through the girl. His house was later searched, the picture found and he arrested. He was never seen again. His clinic was burnt down and his family disinherited.

I listened in shocked amazement at a revelation which made me look like a real saint in hell. Dr. Nigonle had one last revelation.

"When it was rumoured that students in the U.S. were trying to form an opposition wing out there, I was commissioned to destroy them. When the names and addresses of the students were given to me I faked a spy package which I sent to each of them which created the impression that they had been sent out there on a spy mission to the U.S. I caused the information to leak to the U.S. Government. The students were immediately deported. Of course we were waiting for them at the airport." Here he paused in genuine compunction for a whole minute and then said: "I honestly do not know where they are now. I hate to think that they were killed. Their blood bothers me a lot....

"When I was finally forced to go on retirement, I could not use my professional training which I had abandoned for twenty years because of a lifetime of evil. I suddenly developed a dislike for young and successful people. I detested young and beautiful girls especially because they saw me as too old for their company. I sought the slightest opportunity to disgrace and hurt them. I held everybody hostage because I tried to know only unpleasant things about them. They said I had a bad mouth. And then I heard of Our Father, and came and listened to him, and he has led me to Jesus, in whom I have found another home. I have another fellowship in Jesus...."

***

The third disclosure sounded even more odious in my ears. It was made by Brother Ngangsaw Abegnogo, alias "Stone," by virtue of his hard-heartedness. He had begun as a mechanic in a garage in Bali. Under cover of darkness he stole a vehicle given to them for repairs to go on "clando" along the Widikum road. He was involved in an accident in which three people died. Unrecognised he escaped back and slept, claiming ignorance the next day when the theft was discovered. When he noticed that he was gradually being suspected he decided to escape. But, having no money he decided to waylay students from the college going to town or returning to the campus. Under the influence of a pinch of hemp he took, he was able to surrender three students, two boys and a girl. He squeezed 5000 francs from the boys. When one of them seemed to recognise him, and to confuse their reasoning faculties, he compelled them at gunpoint to smoke hemp also. After they had done so he undressed them and made them flee back to school naked and mad with the hemp they had been forced to smoke. He had then raped the girl. He disclosed that the girl was later pregnant, attempted an abortion and died in the process.

74

ⁿⁿⁿⁿⁿⁿⁿⁿⁿⁿⁿⁿ

His second sin was just as blood curdling: he had then joined a second division football team in the far eastern province. Aspiring to enter the elite First Division with ease they had resorted to the consultation of oracles and secret societies. One medicine man who swore he could do the trick for them had asked for the tongue of an unborn child. This, he, as the captain of the team had brought, killing an innocent pregnant mother working peacefully on her farm in the process. In spite of all these risks, his club had not only failed to enter the First Division, but had descended into the Third Division. The weight of his crimes had threatened to crush him, even though he had not at any one moment been detected as the perpetrator. He had gone up to the police to report himself, but because it looked like imprisonment would please him, the police had asked for a bribe. He had not given.

"The blood of all the people I killed worried me like a bone in my throat," he ended up. "Then I heard of A.L.C.A. And then I came to a Crusade and then to the church and met Our Father and asked him to help me, and he promised to lead me to God. And he did, and he has asked me to pledge my life in the service of The Colony that he may intercede for God to forgive me. I now have another home in him...."

My own confession came as an anticlimax to the evening's event, and I am sure that after listening to me some may have secretly wondered why I came there at all.

Chapter Fourteen

Dennis Nunqam Ndendemajem

In keeping with the spirit of ALCA, another Gospel Crusade was planned for Ngeashia, a small town about seventy kilometres out of Menako sub-division. All week long the radio talked about the event, mentioning the names of the speakers and performers. The public was especially delighted to hear that Mammy Nyanga was going to lead her famous choir, and that Uncle Benz was going to animate.

Pastor Shrapnell struck the best bargain in town when he won over to our church, Uncle Benz. He was a popular singer and entertainer who had several sophisticated musical instruments which bereaved families usually hired during funerals and death celebrations. Uncle Benz accompanied us on this crusade during which he was the principal animator.

The Colony bus took the full load of 17 passengers together with the entire paraphernalia of Uncle Benz's mobile musical studio. We arrived Ngeashia at 4 p.m. two hours before the Crusade was due to kick off and immediately set about preparing the place. Earlier in the day a messenger had been sent to supervise the erecting of a stage for the performance. Two gigantic loud speakers were mounted, one on each side of the stage such that the speaker could be heard from about a kilometre away. To the right of the stage was a large table on which Uncle Benz set up his portable piano, electric xylophone and turn-table.

A pulpit was then set up in the centre of the stage. With the help of cables from the Colony they were able to tap electric current from a nearby petrol station and then surround the whole area with 100 watts bulbs.

***

At six o'clock precisely , the music which had been booming for about an hour stopped. Reverend Pastor Shrapnell mounted the stage from behind the scenes. He was flanked by the four main speakers for the evening, including Brother Toby, the interpreter, and then a choir of eight: two blind, two lame, two deaf and two dwarfs.

Brother Toby, virtually the master of ceremony introduced the key speakers. Pastor Shrapnell led the opening prayer and then withdrew to his chair behind the Rostrum. The no more than one metre tall Mammy Nyanga darted across the stage to the delight of everybody, curtsied and then intoned the opening song:

He who has found Jesus...

She raised her right stump of an arm: "One two three, go," her wiry voice rang out. Our choir of freaks began, each group responding according to his or her own infirmity:

He who has found Jesus
He who has found Jesus,
though he has no eyes, sees
He who has lost Jesus,
though he has eyes, sees not; though he
has ears, hears not; though he has legs runs not;
For Jesus is the eye,
Jesus is the ear, Jesus is the legs....

First to speak after the rousing opening song was "Blackboard", the blind entertainer. He thanked and praised Pastor Shrapnell "Our Father" for leading him to God and that he now saw clearly the power of God having turned his defect into advantage. He could now weave baskets and even read Braille and play the organ.

"Bundle" the lame man praised God and Shrapnell that thanks to them he could now run faster than an antelope.

"Ex-Service," Sister Rebecca, the divorcee, spoke of marriage. Marriage to man, she said was a pact of a season. "It is when you are married to Christ that you are truly married because you are married forever," she ended up.

Pastor Shrapnell's was the turning point of the evening. As though under the influence of some spirits he held the crowd spell bound for one full hour and a half. Fearlessly, and with perspiration running down his face he shouted at the crowd, quoting endlessly from Genesis to Revelation. I could not believe what I was seeing. There were three different Bibles before him, but he did not as much as open any. He would pick up one and holding it close to the people and then quote a text to them before putting it down and picking up another. With absolute impunity he castigated the iniquity of the politicians whom he stigmatized as vultures, who have converted a once joyously floating ship of state into a sinking vessel.

"The end is near," he shouted. "Listen, more disasters have visited mankind out of the fact that they refused to listen than any other single cause." He quoted Adam and Eve who refused to listen to God's commandment. He quoted the captain of the apparently unsinkable ship, **The Titanic** which drowned in 1912, the engineer of the New York building that was later called the **Towering Inferno**...." Without any fear whatsoever he castigated Government leaders all over the world for wanting to die in power, by rigging elections, creating phantom polling stations, intimidating political opponents and even killing others, all in the name of Democracy. "America, the so-called cradle of Democracy, is no exception," he shouted. He drew attention to something he called **CREEP** - the **Committee for the Re-election of President Nixon**. That, he said was the organization that brought to the attention of the public *THE WATERGATE SCANDAL* that caused Americans so much shame. In fact he attacked every known vice, his hands sweeping the hall in broad mock accusation that made each of us wonder for a while if we were indeed free from his charges.

People were both moved and impressed and responded encouragingly. When the baskets were sent round for contributions the sum of 97,000 francs was realised. Even more than this, 11 people pledged their lives at the service of The Colony.

***

On our return to The Colony I could not conceal my admiration for Pastor Shrapnell. "It was unbelievable, Our Father," I said to him after prayers the following morning. "I am looking forward to the day when I can win the hearts of so many people on a single day by talking about God."

"Faith can move mountains," Pastor Shrapnell said. "With time, with hard work and with trust in God, you can win the world to God's side."

It was on this occasion that I made the move that endeared me to Pastor Shrapnell as never before. Although Pastor Shrapnell had made a monumental effort to learn pidgin English and was able to communicate with many of the uneducated converts and aspiring followers, he could not sustain a discourse of the type he delivered during Crusades. Accordingly he always travelled with an interpreter, through whom he delivered his sermons.

Brother Toby was his acknowledged interpreter. He knew much about the Bible and quoted extensively from it. But he knew it more out of memorization than careful understanding. He was energetic and sincere and tried as much as possible to interpret as accurately as possible. But because he generally had problems keeping pace with the speed with which Shrapnell spoke, the result was that many of his renditions from Pastor Shrapnell's Americanisms into pidgin English were inaccurate, sometimes downright wrong. On a good number of cases interpretations of solemn deliveries had drawn chuckles instead of silent nods.

Many people had always noticed that there something wrong with the interpretation, but many were not bold enough to draw attention to it because they could not replace Brother Toby. I was the first to draw attention to it and offer a solution.

"I have nothing against Brother Toby," I told him. "He has many limitations. My point is that for the efforts that you are making to save souls and bring happiness to every heart, it is important that the listeners receive the message the way it ought to be received. I think I can serve A.L.C.A. better than Brother Toby in that respect."

I quite remembered Pastor Shrapnell's first sermon I listened to in which he spoke of St Francis of Assissi abandoning riches to join God. I quite remembered Pastor saying "Henceforth he decided to build the house of God..." I quite remembered how lost I was for a while when Brother Toby interpreted "Henceforth" as "Hens fought." He said "even hens fought with St. Francis to build the church of God."

I quoted a few instances of embarrassing misinterpretations to prove this argument just from the apparently very successful Ngeashia Crusade.

There was first the point when Pastor Shrapnell was talking about openness before God during prayer.

"Do not assume that God knows everything in your heart" he said. "Tell him frankly, for you cannot cheat God." And to emphasize the point he said:

"You cannot rob God!"

Brother Toby's interpretation was interesting. "If you have any francs tell God," he said. And as for robbing God he asked "If God stood in front of you and asked you to rub him how can you when you do not know the kind of oil he rubs?"

When Shrapnell quoted from the Old Testament concerning the foretelling of the coming of Christ he quoted the verse which said : "Behold the handmaid of the Lord.."

Brother Toby interpreted it as "he held the hand made by God...," an interpretation which drew laughter from some listeners.

By far the most bizarre was the interpretation of the parable of the Good Samaritan in which he said "rubber trees fell on the traveller," and that the Good Samaritan took his Axe of the Apostles and cut the trees and freed the unfortunate traveller.

I did one interpretation in the Colony and thereafter I was the official interpreter of A.L.C.A.

Chapter Fifteen

Madam Gertrude

This world is not our home. We are just passing through. It is such a small place. So small that you should be making friends, not enemies, because you do not know who will save you tomorrow. When you are doing something you should know that one day you will have to answer for it. I don't mean during the last judgment. I mean on earth here. If I knew that I would ever meet Mr. Dennis again on this earth, I would have behaved differently towards him. On the 18th of August, it might have been about six months after I parted from Mr. Dennis, I parked my things from my parents' compound and decided that I would go and join a few of my friends who, having separated from their husbands were living there happily.

I took a taxi to the Colony. It was about 3 o'clock in the afternoon. Even before the taxi stopped outside the gate I could see a thin man walking up and down, reading a paper book or something of the sort. As soon as the taxi halted and I came out at the entrance, the taxi driver opened his own door and went to the boot and took down my large valise.

I straightened my down-reaching green gown which I was wearing, adjusted my white head scarf and clasped my handbag under my armpit in readiness to carry my bag myself. Apparently the thin man reading his book noticed that I was coming to stay there and, interrupting his reading, came up and offered to help me. Without paying too much attention to him I let him carry the bag with thanks. I did not ask him any questions. I was still thinking of how I was going to start talking. He had barely taken three steps ahead of me when something struck me.

"Mr. Dennis Nunqam!" I exclaimed. "What are you doing here?" I asked. I told myself that I had walked into my own trap.

He let the heavy bag rest slowly on the ground, turned round, looked at me and also exclaimed:

"Madam Gertrude! Madam Essemo! Madam Max! I should be the one to ask you why you are here. I have been here, madam, since..."

My blood ran cold. I was sure that he was going to say he had been living there since I drove him from my house. He did not say so, which made me feel relieved.

I looked nervously at him for a whole tense minute and then said:

"I can carry that bag myself." I was very ashamed of myself, knowing what I had done to this man before. In fact, if the taxi had not driven off immediately I took down my bag, I would have fled back rather than confront Mr. Dennis.

He seemed to have read my thoughts because he told me at once: "Don't worry, madam, let me help you."

***

He led me through the Salvation Colony main gate into the waiting area. There he very respectfully showed me where to sit and personally went in to talk to Pastor Shrapnell. As I sat there I was wondering what he would be telling the Pastor. I could imagine him telling the Pastor how I used to laugh at him, how I used to give him my inner wears to wash, and things of the sort.

Luckily for me there was somebody sitting with me who kept reassuring me that I would be well received. He kept asking me all sorts of questions about my life. When Mr. Dennis came out the man went in and was with the Pastor for some time before I was called in. I was not anxious to talk to Mr. Dennis until I had known what he had told the Pastor about me. He too, when he noticed that I was not anxious to talk to him he simply kept quiet, which reminded me of the bad old days. That was how he used to sit. I remember Dr. Eshuonti describing him as a pond, one unmoved by excitement of any sort.

When I was shown the way into the Pastor's office, I was unsure of many things. I had come ready to take up permanent residence in The Colony, but in the light of the fact that Mr. Dennis too was there, a man to whom I had done so much harm, I expected that after having spoken about me, the Pastor would walk up to me and order me to go back. What a disgrace that would be!

What happened next surprised me. The Pastor showed me where to sit, which I did nervously.

"Madam Gertrude," he called as if he had known me for ages.

"You are welcome to this Colony."

I thanked him and looked on.

"Brother Dennis has told me all about you," he began.

I put my hand to my mouth.

"Do not be worried that you have run into Brother Dennis here," he said. "He started speaking of you from the first day he came here. In this Colony we live like brothers and sisters, having forgiven everybody who trespassed against us."

I readjusted my sitting position in great relief. He told me even more than I knew about myself. He told me of the people who had hurt me and also those I had hurt and encouraged me to consider them all forgiven.

"The spirit of this Colony is to forgive us our trespasses as we forgive them that trespass against us," he concluded. I immediately vowed to forgive everybody. He said in the next SOUL TO SOUL which was to come in two days I would be called upon to reconcile with my enemies, especially Brother Dennis. I had never heard of SOUL TO SOUL. But he explained the whole thing to me and I was anxious to be part of it.

I was shown my cubicle in the women's hall by three ladies who were described as Brethren's Keepers. I looked forward to the SOUL TO SOUL with great anticipation. It was during my encounter with them that I learned what the Pastor had said to me, that they called him Our Father.

***

This particular Soul-to-Soul, as Our Father told me the next day, was to be of a very special significance because it was the first time I was coming face to face with Mr. Dennis. Even more than this, it was only the third time two former enemies were meeting in The Colony. That Friday evening, Our Father asked Brother Dennis to talk first.

"Twice I have told you of a certain lady whose conduct drove me to want to hang myself," Brother Dennis began. "Soul to Soul, E-i-men!" he cried.

"E-i-men!" everybody answered back. Had I not been thoroughly briefed on what to expect, I would simply have walked me away from the horrible exposure. But the people were not even looking at me.

"After all that she did to me and against me, what did I say that I may rest in perfect peace and tranquillity in the kingdom of the Lord?"

"Forgiveness!" they all shouted.

Our Father himself stepped forward and took me by the hand back to the podium and said:

"Sister Gertrude, stand here and pour forth the bitterness of thy heart that you may find perfect peace and tranquillity in the kingdom of God. Even as it was written: Mark chapter 11 verses 25 and 26:

Whenever you stand praying, if you have anything against anyone, forgive him, that your father in heaven may also forgive you your trespasses.'

But if you do not forgive, neither will your father in heaven forgive you your trespasses.'"

I touched my green scarf over my low hair, straightened my green blouse that ended at the elbow, and which I had caused the tailor to stitch so that it would hide my very large breasts. I moved to the edge of the dais, pulled up my pink skirt which reached down to my ankles and jumped down. I took a few steps towards the first row of anxious listeners. There I began my confession which many people praised me for several months afterwards.

"If Mr. Dennis had hanged himself," I began, "it was me who caused it all. Everything that he has said about me and against me is true." I paused briefly. I could feel the weight of my heavy hands which I clasped over my bulging belly. I unclasped my right hand and used the back to wipe my mouth.

"But why did I do what I did?"

I lowered my voice conspiratorially. "My husband," I shouted, my voice rising to a suddenly high pitch, what we called in the choir **crescendo**. "That man they call Max, he will not see eye-to-eye with me. If I say rain is falling he will say the sun is shining. Not even that, he would want me to stand in public and refuse what everybody else saw to be true."

I pointed in Brother Dennis's direction and said: "Only God alone knows what Mr. Dennis did to him that he should be the only one Dr. Max would want to see in the house. My husband refused my junior brothers and sisters from coming to live in the house, even though they were dying of hunger in the village. Only Mr. Dennis.

"So before Mr. Dennis ever came I had made up my mind that if my husband did not first bring my own relatives to live with me and enjoy my sweat, I would make sure that that his Mr. Dennis did not set foot in my house. Or if he entered he would have one foot outside."

"Does it mean that brother Dennis never offended you directly in any way?" somebody inquired in the middle row.

"If what I am saying is a lie, let me cut my tongue..."

"Don't swear," Our Father cautioned me.

"Mr. Dennis never did anything to me," I replied loudly. "I did all that to him just to hurt and annoy my husband."

"So how do you feel towards brother Dennis now?" one of the Keepers asked.

I ran up to Mr. Dennis, went on my knees and said:

"If papa God is listening, let him ask Mr. Dennis to pardon..."

Brother Dennis stepped forward.

"Alleluia!" he said.

"Praise the Lord," the others answered.

Pointing to me he said: "I had said it before in her absence, and I am now saying it in her presence. Sister Gertrude, that we may live in perfect peace and tranquillity in God's Kingdom now and forever, I forgive you with all my heart, everything you did to me, and even the ones you were still planning to do when I took my rope..."

"E-i-men!"

"E-i-men!"

Mr. Dennis then resumed his seat. Now feeling a lot more relieved I was bent on pouring forth my heart.

"And why am I here now?" I asked. "The bad things I have done were too much. All of them against my husband. We women," I shook my head. "God made us but spoiled us again. When I heard in 196... that I was going to meet my husband in Italy, I said to myself, let me take the last dose, as we called it. I went to my boyfriend..."

There was a slight chuckle.

"Yes, na, who did not have a boyfriend in those days?. I had been preventing pregnancy year by year. I now wanted to make sure that I could still deliver. When I missed my period I was happy because I was going to meet my husband."

There was a hush. I looked round with a touch of embarrassment. Our Father urged me on as if he was really deriving some particular satisfaction from my revelation. He urged me on. On my part, the more I revealed about myself, the better I felt.

"Then my husband wrote changing the date of my leaving to go and meet him. He added six weeks. So the belly which I had hoped to hide and enter his house with began to swell minute minute. I was determined not to remove it. So I went to Italy with it. My husband received me well well. I thought he did not know what had happened. For seven years I never thought he knew it. Five months ago, when Mr. Dennis tried to hang himself, he told me about that pregnancy."

"Oh no!" somebody complained.

"You see my brothers and sisters, why I say that my husband is a very bad man," I threw my hands helplessly at them and went on. "You do something wrong, a man knows about it, but he does not mention it for seven years?"

The listeners nodded.

"Then as I was living with him he paid no attention to me as a man would take care of his wife..."

"But were you really his wife?" somebody inquired, but I knew from the spirit of the event that his intention was not to hurt me.

"Whosai," another said.

"Peace, be still!" Brother Dennis raised a hand.

"It is only five months ago that I knew he was treating me like a stick because he knew that he was not the father of our first child. He gave me money and bought me everything that I asked him to buy, let me not tell a lie. But was I married to his money and the things he bought?"

"Whosai!" somebody answered.

"I wanted my husband whom I was married to," I said sadly. "He denied me, he turned his back on me. So I made a mistake."

"Again?" somebody asked.

"Yes, again," I admitted, smiled to myself, mopped my face, moved closer to the edge of the dais. "Sitting in the house alone, curious to be satisfied, and listening to stories about things my friends did to help themselves, I tried something with Bakru, my husband's driver."

There was some whistling from the middle row.

"Soul to Soul, E-i-men!" another shouted.

"E-e-i-i-men!" the rest answered.

"Go befo."

"The bad news is that my husband knew that too. It seems like he knew everything before I started thinking about it. That too he did not make me feel that he knew about it until five months ago when brother Dennis climbed to the ceiling with his rope..."

"There was no ceiling in the room," Mr. Dennis cut in humorously.

"So they say if there is no ceiling you should hang?" somebody asked.

There was a brief laugh and then I went on:

"So when Brother Dennis hanged himself and he said all these things to me which I thought I was hiding, I was frightened because I did not know what else he knew about me which he was waiting for another occasion to reveal.

"He drove me from the house. And I told myself that before I left I would do something to hurt him more and more. I took our second child's hand and as I went out he shouted: 'You witch, leave my child behind.' That was when I made the third mistake."

"Again and again?"

I smiled and cleaned my face. "I will tell you all," I said.

"Go befo."

"Can you ever deliver a beautiful child like this? I asked. Don't touch Bakru's child," I told him."

There was a long pause.

"And do you know how satan destroys somebody?"

Silence.

"It was not Bakru's child. It was my husband's child, and poor Bakru was sitting in the parlour, hearing all. My husband had just been insulting me to his hearing. And the poor man was sitting there hearing, unable to refuse, unable to run away."

The silence persisted.

"And as I am talking to you now, brothers and sisters, Bakru is still in jail. He has not been tried. He will not be tried. He will simply die there because he was put there by a man as big as Dr. Maximillian Essemo."

Our Father smiled the way I was to discover he usually did when he saw people baffled by a problem which he could very easily solve.

"And what does Sister Gertrude want to see done, that she may live in perfect peace and tranquillity in the kingdom of the Lord?"

"Our Father, I want Bakru brought here that we may confess our guilt together."

"And for your husband what do you offer?"

I bit my lips, and squeezed my eyes until tears ran down, but said nothing.

"Say, sister Gertrude, that you have forgiven your husband all that he has done, that you may..."

I screamed.

***

It was only during the second and third SOUL TO SOUL that I was able to voice my forgiveness of Dr. Essemo. And even then, I only did so after Our Father had assured me that he would use his position as the man of God to get Bakru a reprieve and a release.

This he easily did, and before Dr. Essemo knew of it Bakru had spent three months in Salvation Colony with us.

Chapter Sixteen

Cosmas Mfetebeunu

The thought had been on my mind since the first day I arrived from Nigeria. I mean the thought that it would be wrong for me to sit back and see my sister's husband abandon his marital home to follow a religion of charlatans. I told myself from that first day that I would get him out of it, by hook or crook, especially by crook! But to do this I needed to understand precisely what had actually happened to my brother in-law. My sister first telephoned to Dr. Essemo with whom my in-law, Dennis lived before running away to join ALCA. I later encouraged her to give me a letter to Dr. Essemo in Menako introducing myself.

***

Dr. Essemo told me everything about Dennis whom he stressed was once his friend, but was no longer and was never to be again. He told me he was not interested in knowing where Dennis was, and did not care a thing about whatever happened to him thereafter. I could see he hated what Mr. Dennis had tried to do in his house.

Since it was a lot nearer, from Menako I decided to pay a visit to the Salvation Colony. Mr. Dennis had never met me before, but as Manda told me, he knew me well well from conversations with her, from conversations within my family circle and then from my pictures and letters.

He received me outside the gate into The Colony. When he came out to meet me, it took me quite a while to reconcile his looks with those of the man whose pictures I had in my album. He looked so terribly thin with an elongated or a crane-like neck which was accentuated by the fact that he was a tall person by nature. In a word, he looked very unimpressive physically.

His hair on his head was low and his beard though also low, was not quite neatly kept. He had high cheekbones which by virtue of the abstemious life he had led recently protruded above his shrunken jaws, giving his eyes below his hooded brows a sunken faraway look.

His hands were thin, so were his fingers and toes which showed through the pair of cheap second-hand sandals he was wearing. He looked a lot older than I had been given to believe. If he did not assure me that he was in very good health, I would have sworn that he had some lung problems.

He was wearing a simple jumpa made from the cheapest material - *CICAM*, and which gave his thin neck an elongated or crane-like shape. He was also wearing a cheap second-hand pair of trousers.

***

I was holding an over-used eighty-leaves exercise book which I folded.

"I am Cosmas Mfetebeunu," I introduced myself rather hesitantly because he did not look excited at anything. "I am the elder brother of Manda Chabeule, does the name ring a bell, sir?" I inquired.

"It does, brother," he said calmly.

"In what sense does it ring a bell?" I asked further.

"Manda is my wife," he said with the same lack of emotion. I went straight into the matter that had brought me there.

"I expected you to say she **was** your wife, not **is** your wife," I said.

He looked at me and then asked: "Brother Cosmas, what makes you say so? Why would you want to put words into my mouth?"

"Because I don't see how you would call a woman your wife whom you have abandoned with your three children for a whole year," I blasted.

"Two children," he corrected me.

I could see a fluttering of twinkles in his left eye. I chose not to press the point further. I recalled how hesitant my sister had always been to talk about the third child.

"God be praised, brother Cosmas," he said. "Your sister always talked to me about you. Thanks be to God. How are they?"

I looked at him and he looked at me, but there was no response. I had wanted to tell him: "If you were a responsible husband you should not be the one to ask me. You should be telling me about your family."

But the total politeness and calmness with which he spoke, coupled with the fact that I had so much to discuss with him made me keep quiet. I preferred to persuade rather than bully him out of the place.

"So you have been studying in Nigeria?" he asked.

"Yes, I have been studying in Nigeria," I responded.

"Praise the Lord," he nodded and asked "What were you studying?"

"I did a B.A. in Journalism and a diploma in Mass Communication."

"The Lord be thanked that he has brought you safely back," he said, "for all life belongs to Jesus. You see, brother Cosmas, that the Lord loves you?"

I shrugged.

"I would like you to convince me about this place," I said. "You threw away a golden opportunity to have made your life comfortable. A man invited you and gave you everything..."

"He did not give me everything, brother Cosmas," he said in the same offensively calm manner. "Only one person can give anybody everything. And that one person is God. Dr. Essemo was no God. He was just a rich man. And like all rich men, he made no effort to understand the world of a poor friend."

I could feel my eyes roll in my head. I hated to have this man convince me about any line of action that he had taken. And yet what he had said was so frightfully true.

"He did not need to," I persisted. "You were poor, were you not?"

"I was."

"He was rich, was he not?"

"He was. I was poor, not mad," Mr. Dennis said. "If Dr. Essemo really wanted to help me, he should have looked for an opportunity to talk to me personally, to ask me what I can really do and how he could help me realise that goal within my own limits. This he did not do. He announced it to my entire family that he wanted to make me a doctor. And just because I had nothing, nobody thought I was worth listening to. They held meetings behind my back, arranged with my wife and my in-laws to ship me to Menako. Brother Cosmas, that was not right. I was not the poorest man on the planet. That was what destroyed me."

When he finished talking there was a very long hollow silence. My indignation was, against my wish, gradually turning to sympathy. At least although I had come because I was disappointed in his actions, I was not so angry as to deny that what he was saying made sense. He may have a case after all, I thought.

I drew in a long breath and asked: "But if you went there and found the going tough, why not go back to Mbongo?"

"Mbongo? It looked as if, if I did not become a doctor I should not return there."

I looked appalled by what he was saying. "Did anybody actually say so?" I asked.

"I am no child, Brother Cosmas," he said. "They did not have to say so. It was clear in their every action..."

"And they say you tried to hang yourself. You would have died..."

"I would have died, but I did not," he said decisively. "If I died, it would have been the will of God. But since I did not die, it was His will still. Now I see why he could never have allowed me to die. I was living in the dark. He could not have allowed me to die in the dark. He has shown me the light, the light of Jesus. And now that I have seen the light..."

I had not gone there to be converted but to convince him to leave the place. It was beginning to look like he would convert me. I was bent on showing him the hollowness of his philosophy. "If you have really seen the light as you claim," I began, "how come that you cannot see your wife, your parents, your children? That your light does not reach them?"

"The light shineth in the darkness but the darkness comprehendeth it not," he said imperturbably and dived straight into the scriptures in which he seemed to be soaked. "According to the Gospel according to Luke 14 verse 26, our Lord says: *If anyone comes to me and does not hate his father and mother, wife and children, brother and sisters, yes, and his own life also, he cannot be my disciple.* E-i-men."

"E-i-men," I came close to saying. There was something hypnotic in his words.

"Well, Moyo Dennis," I said a bit more persuasively, "the main reason I have come here today is because I feel hurt by the fact that my sister has been abandoned at such an early age. And you know that when you leave a woman to herself, there are so many things she can do that will not be exactly pleasing to the eyes of concerned relatives."

"Did your sister say that I divorced her?" he asked me.

"What you did was worse than divorce," I told him. "Had you told her that you did not want her, it would even have been better. You just took off, knowing that she was expecting your third child. It is not done."

He looked startled for a brief second.

"Did you say I left Manda pregnant?" he inquired.

"Of course," I said. "Why do you think I am so worried? Your baby girl whom you have not seen is one year old today."

"That child is not my child," Mr. Dennis said calmly.

My blood ran cold.

"Ask Dr. Essemo whose baby it is," he said. "She is not my child. She is not my child."

I had been standing by the tree to the right of the gate. I was so stunned that I had to sit down on a huge white-washed stone under the tree before finally mustering the wit to talk. I tried to speak but checked myself and, instead, cleaned my mouth with the back of my left hand and remained silent.

If the baby was not Mr. Dennis' baby, then whose was it? I wondered. Could Mr. Dennis be right in declaring at once that it was Dr. Essemo's baby?

Chapter Seventeen

Cosmas Mfetebeunu

It took me an awfully long time to discover that Mr. Dennis was absolutely ignorant of whatever transpired between my sister and Dr. Essemo after he left them. He did not care about them. He had embraced his new religion with one mind and told himself often: "No man having put his hand on the plough and looking back is fit for the kingdom of heaven."

Although at the time Mr. Dennis was talking to me he did not actually mean that it was Dr. Essemo who had fathered the child, Dr. Essemo was indeed the father of the child! It all began very harmlessly, like a joke. As I would learn years afterwards, my sister spent 6 weeks at Dr. Essemo's place after the disappearance of Dennis. Dr. Essemo found my sister most serviceable. She worked indefatigably all over the house, mopping the floor, weeding the garden and flower beds, cooking food, washing and ironing clothes. It was not in Dr. Essemo's nature to go out hunting for girls or free women.

He had, over the years cultivated the habit of spending his evenings at home or in his office. The thought of what Mr. Dennis had done to their two families was never to leave his mind. He never failed to pity my sister and to curse Dennis. I was to learn that one day as they sat together in the parlour he exclaimed:

"Why did God make things like this?"

"Like what, doctor?" my sister asked.

"Giving a good woman like you to a cow like Dennis and giving me a Jezebel like Gertrude!" he added.

My sister looked at Dr. Essemo for a while and then said with calculated suggestiveness:

"But have they not gone away, Doctor?"

Dr. Essemo shook his head in disappointment. He saw in my sister a young woman starved of the pleasures of marriage, through no fault of hers. On her part, she too felt the same way about Dr. Essemo. She wondered why a nice man like Dr. Essemo was made to marry an obnoxious woman like Gertrude. She pitied Dr. Essemo that at that young age he should spend his time alone.

Here were two adults who until lately had been separately married. They had both *lost* their partners, and it would be wrong to think that the thought of belonging to each other now never crossed their minds.

This community of feeling became so strong that one night when Dr. Essemo returned from town after having taken a lot of alcohol, he strolled into my sister's room and, as if she was already his wife, made love to her. The following morning, coming to himself he tendered an unnecessary apology. It was not a case of seduction because he did what she was most happy to do. Not that she was promiscuous in any way. The two had counted Dennis out of the human society. Dr. Essemo who was so glad to see him leave his residence unhurt, did not give him more than a week before he hung or drowned himself. He did not see how things could turn round and bring Dennis back into the society of normal human beings.

My sister thought no less. In fact, she usually spoke of Mr. Dennis as "my late husband!" Although on such occasions she actually wanted to say "my former husband," it reflected how lightly she thought of her relationship with Mr. Dennis. The sex act in itself was seen on both sides as a benevolent gesture. It was its aftermath which complicated the matter. In the first place, Dr. Essemo repeated the act three times, without even the excuse of alcohol. On the third occasion he warned her to inform him if she noticed any signs of pregnancy and he would perform a D & C on her.

Anxious to have a child (her husband had repeatedly discouraged her from sharing the same bed with him for a whole year!) and lucky to find herself in a position to have one by a man so great as Dr. Essemo she hid her pregnancy from him. As a matter of fact, it was fear of discovery that prompted her to return to Mbongo. Dr. Essemo took the news of the pregnancy very unkindly, but was soon comforted when my sister assured him that she had already told her people that Mr. Dennis shared the bed with her just before he turned bad.

***

It would take me five years to learn of this. But at the time, acting in ignorance I tried to defend my sister.

"I did not hate Manda," Mr. Dennis resumed. "I do not hate her even now. I hate nobody. It is written, Matthew chapter 5 verse 44:... *pray for those who persecute you, so that you may become the sons of your father in heaven. For he makes his sun to shine on bad and good people alike, and gives rain to those who do good and to those who do evil.*

"But I will never forget that she was in the forefront of the forces that came to destroy me. A force which took no account of what I was. A force that came to destroy my real self and remould it in its own image.

"Look at me, Brother Cosmas," he threw his hands open. Can you make me a doctor? Can I ever drive a Mercedes car? Can I ever earn millions which my friends earned? Can I ever build storey buildings? Do I need to be a doctor? Do I need to earn millions? Do I need to build skyscrapers? Can everybody have everything?"

"As I was saying, Moyo Dennis," I stepped in, "what has actually brought me here is my sister's plight. You get married to a woman, you have children with her, and then you suddenly abandon them...."

"I am married to Jesus," he said. "Any other marriage is of the flesh. I am bound to Christ our Lord who suffered on the cross, died and was buried for our sins...."

He seemed impervious to any persuasion. "I do not particularly care about why he died or whether he was thrown in a stream or tied to an electric pole," I told him. It was impossible not to lose one's patience with such a blockhead! I went on:

"My worry is why you would disown your family to follow Christ who was such a family man. Read the Bible again, which has become your breakfast, lunch and supper, Mr Dennis, and you will see that Christ did not cut himself off from his family. All his disciples were very married, with children..."

He smiled the kind of knowing smile that seemed to suggest that I was talking in unawareness. "Matthew 27,45," he quoted. *"Eli, Eli, Lema sabachthani? My God My God, Why hast thou foresakened me?"*

He leaned over me sitting on the stone and placed his right hand patronisingly on my shoulder and said: "Dennis Nunqam Ndendemajem is not the first man of God to..."

"Mr Dennis," I interrupted, "don't follow the shadow and lose the real thing. These churches that you are carrying on your head, are all branches of business. The representative of every single church on this planet is a business magnate. Those who come out here are heavily sponsored from abroad. Those who lead from within this country live in total luxury. Just look round. Visit the home of the Bishop of the catholic church, or the home of a simple priest from the poorest parents; visit the Moderator of the Presbyterian church, the pastor of any of the sects around. They milk the poor dry to feed fat on the pretext that they are preparing you for better days after death.

102

"If you have not gone into this because you have something to gain in concrete financial terms, then you have just wasted your time. No white man comes here to save the African. He comes here because he has something to gain personally from talking to you about God."

Mr. Dennis looked across at me and then shook his head as if to say "this man is still living in the dark."

"Let me be very honest with you moyo," I pressed on. "These churches or sects are nothing new to me. I was a member of the Pentecostal Evangelists for 8 years in Calabar. And how did I get in? I got in simply because I saw that by carrying a bible every Sunday and reciting a few verses of the Bible I was sure of my tuition fees every term.

"The resident pastor was married with two wives, ran a poultry, a piggery and a fishpond..."

"We have all that and more...." Mr. Dennis broke in.

"He was sponsoring two girls, one in the University of Benin and the other in the University of Ahmadu Bello...."

Mr. Dennis seemed determined on disproving me.

"We are sponsoring whole villages," he said.

That did not mean a thing to me. "Two years after he arrived in Nigeria," I continued, "he won the Evangelist of the Year Award Medal. His wives and children were there to give him flowers of congratulations and take pictures to celebrate the occasion. Don't tell me God was not or is still not behind him."

"ALCA is different from your church, Brother Cosmas," he said unruffled. "Our Father is our saviour. He brings joy to the sad, heals the sick, makes the blind to see, the deaf to hear, the lame to walk..."

I laughed a long and deliberately deprecating laugh.

"How can a man of your calibre be so totally deceived? Moyo Dennis," I asked. "Take this letter from your wife and read," I said.

"You have read it?" he asked.

"I have not," I denied. "I have said your wife is my sister."
He took it, tore it open and read it to the end.

My Dear Husband;
I hope that this few words of mind will find you in a good condition of health there in that your church home there.
I did not know that you will just abandon all of us like you have done, your own wife and your own children, weather it is because of what or because of what, tell us.
We all knew what you did in Dr. Max house was not good. That is why I did not answer you and did not want to listen to anything from you. But is that the reason why you will just run away from your home like that? Even if it was what or what, you will just run?
Please return back to us We want to see you. You should see us too. I am so confuse now, I don't know what to say.

Good bye.
Manda, your wife, and your children too.

He folded it and put it back in the envelope and placed the envelope aside.

"I have read it," he said mechanically, and without the slightest show of emotion.

I was determined to convince him to see the need to visit Mbongo. I did not think it necessary to dwell on the letter if he did not think it important. In the end he seemed somehow to yield to the pressure. What he said next made me feel encouraged. He said:

"If I am going there it is not because I miss my children. I have children here, brothers, sisters..."

That was already a monstrous concession, I thought. But it was not enough. "They are not yours, moyo Dennis," I said. "That is the point I am trying to make you see...

"The children of God are one family," he said. "If I go to Mbongo it is to help my wife and the children and all other people see the light. Our Father was planning a

Crusade for Mbongo for .... I will see how we can arrange
so that it falls earlier. I will go to Mbongo to arrange for the
Crusade. I will also go there and collect my paintings. I want
to go to Ovenga and see whether the American Embassy
can help me exhibit my works. I have some thirty paintings
in the store here."

I was listening once again with growing indignation and
disappointment at the fact that concern for the family was
not amongst his priorities.

"I have some paintings in the house in Mbongo," he said.
"I also have some in Dr. Essemo's place. I have my
manuscripts there also."

"And what will you do with the proceeds after the
exhibition?" I inquired. "I know that such occasions can
fetch money."

"Since I came into this Colony, brother Cosmas," he said,
"I have not done anything to help Our Father. I should be
able to give him money to help the place."

"I don't believe this," I said. "Your family is starving,
you have an opportunity to make money and you want to
give it to a man who has enough already?"

"It is written, brother. *Unto he who has, more shall be added,
and to he who has not, even the little that he has shall be taken away
from ...*"

"Let us forget about that for now. You are coming to
Mbongo, right?"

Mr. Dennis nodded with a confident smile. It was
concluded that he would visit Mbongo, for whatever reason.
I was counting on the fact that the sight of his family would
make him rethink his involvement in the church. In addition
to agreeing to go to Mbongo, I succeeded in getting him to
write a letter to his wife informing her of his impending
homecoming.

Chapter Eighteen

Manda Chabeule

I say this is not gladness that filled my heart when Bro said he had actually seen my husband.

"It is a lie you are lying," I said, just to try him and make sure.

"I spent a whole hour with him," Bro said. "He will be coming here to see you people." He then went into his pocket and took out a letter which he gave me to read. I opened, my hands shaking, fearing that he would ask me about Patricia, the child I know he must have heard that I delivered. Still yet, I was still anxious to hear from him, to hear about him as my husband, no matter what he had done to us. Bro went away. I think he did not want to see how I shall do when I read the letter. So I read the letter.

Dennis Nunqam Ndendemajem
Camp 7, SALVATION COLONY
P.O. Box 123
Menako District
Greater West Province.
3 March, 1973

Dear Manda and the little ones;

May the grace of the Lord be unto you. Tending the flock of the good Lord has kept me away from you a long time. I believe that by God's grace you are all well because without God we are nothing, and with God we are everything. I received this morning Brother Cosmas with whom I discussed very much. There were many things he did not know which I have told him. He will soon see the light of Jesus. I have been in the Colony here with my Brethren in Christ for 13 months and I am glad that my labours are bearing fruit. The kingdom of God is like a mustard seed. When I came here we were 70. Now we are 170. The Lord be praised.

It is happiness without measure to live in the light of Jesus. Due to my intervention ALCA plans a Gospel Crusade to Lebangom in the Mbongo neighbourhood on April 30th. But I will come before that. I shall come to Mbongo to see the Government Delegate to the Urban Council and make arrangements for the location and time. At that time, God willing, I shall see you. That should be on Thursday 23 March, three weeks from today. I shall also see the little ones. I have some small Bibles Stories For Children for them. It will be a good thing for you to attend the Crusade and see the miracle workings of God.

The Lord be with you.

Brother Dennis Ndendemajem.

The joy that was in my heart when I took the letter disappeared. So also did the fear that I was feeling also disappear. My heart became filled with bitter anger. I did not allow my heart to cool down before I reply, so I picked up my pen and wrote back immediately.

My Dear husband;
You are normal? What kind of letter are you writing to me like that? You write to your wife and children you have not seen for one year as if it is the radio talking. You are sick or what? You did not even say you saw the letter I sent, and I know that you saw the letter and read it.

If you want to come, come. After all, for one year we have not died, it is only your coming that will do what? It is you who is running away from your wife, and your children and your house. They are not running from you.

But let me tell you that if you are not coming here to see us, if you are coming here only for that your church crusade, you remain you there because the people here will burn those your church things if you try and come here for that.

I just left the letter like that, no ending. I simply folded it, addressed it and went to the Post Office and threw the nonsense thing into the mail box. I did not tell Bro that I had written because he left him and went him away after he gave me the letter.

***

The day after I wrote to my husband, I said to myself that I should let Dr. Max, my God, know that Dennis had finally written a letter to me. I went to the post office telephone and paid to talk to him. I telephoned his office. He was in. Even without listening for me to tell him what my husband had said in the letter, Dr. Max sounded angry. He warned me:

"If you are carrying on any kind of correspondence with that your mad husband, madam, don't let me know. You know how badly he hurt me."

"I did not write to him, doctor," I begged. He wrote to me." I pleaded.

"Do you have the letter there?" Dr. Max asked.

"I have, doctor."

Dr. Max then asked me to read the letter to him. When I finished reading it over the phone Dr. Max asked:

"Does that sound to you like a human being talking?"

"No, doctor," I said, tears swelling in my throat. I did not know what to do. I felt catarrh in my nose and cough in my throat.

"Madam," he said, "you must be ashamed of having ever been married to such a creature! Did you write back?" he asked.

109

"No, doctor," I lied, tears running down my face and I began to sob. "I could not tell Dr. Max that I had written to Dennis.

"If I were you, madam," he said, "I would never waste my time to reply. If I were you, I would never allow him to touch my children. That your Dennis who was once my friend," he went on, "has long crossed the border of sanity. I am not saying that you should not do what you like... But I warn you that if you allow a ghost to enter your house and anything happens to either your children or your person, you should never apply to me for help. Make up your mind, goodbye."

It was clear, what Dr. Max meant: if I admitted Dennis into my life, I would lose all the favours we were enjoying from him. How could I decide to choose Dennis who had nothing and lose Dr. Maximillian Essemo Aleukwinchaa who had everything?

***

When I left the post office my mind was as if somebody had thrown thorns into it. I went to the right, went to the left and then came back, as if I had taken alcohol. I did not know what to do. Even if I did not lose all the help that we were receiving from Dr. Max, if I accepted Dennis back as my rightful husband, I would have to explain where Patricia came from. To save my face from such disgrace, I had lied to Brother she was Dennis' child. With all this fire burning in my heart I sent a second letter to Dennis. It was just a note:

Dear Dennis;
Please, don't come here again. We don't want to see you, we and the children.

Dennis did not see this note when he left The Colony for Mbongo.

***

I had had all the problems in this world with the children since their father left them. I told them a different story each month, counting on the hope that Dennis would show up any time. When I had Patricia and he still did not show up I told them that he had died.

When I returned from telephoning to Dr. Max I decided to erase Dennis' name from their minds. I told them again that their father had died. Seizing on the word "devil" which Dr. Max had just used I asked my eldest son, Dieudonne:

"Have you ever heard of a ghost?"

"Is a devil," he said.

"If you see a devil or if you see a ghost, what will you do?"

"Run me away."

"Your father died and has returned as a ghost," I said. "If he comes to your school and you allow him to touch you, mmh, you know what will happen to you?"

"We will die," the boy said.

***

I did not stop there. Because Dennis had said in his letter that he would be seeing the children, and for fear that he might go to their school and spoil my children I went there and spoke to the Head Master. I told the man what had happened in my family, how my husband had gone mad, had joined a certain sect and was threatening to come and drag the children into it. I warned him not to allow Dennis to touch the children or speak to them if he ever comes there.

Chapter Nineteen

Ticha Dominique (H. M.)

WHEN YOU travel in public transport, you meet all sorts of queer people! And you are condemned to put up with them until your own journey comes to an end. Try as you can, you are inevitably dragged into their actions, into their lives, for better or for worse. That was exactly what happened on this unfortunate day that I met my man at the South West park. I thought very early in the trip that there was something the matter with him, that he must be one of those obnoxious religious fanatics that had plagued the country.

We were both sitting on the benches waiting for the bus we had chosen to have enough passengers before taking off. The bus needed fourteen passengers to take off, and I was the fourth. My man was the fifth. This meant that we were going to wait for a long time, probably. Two, three or even four hours, depending on how many people may have wanted to travel at that time. He looked high-spirited, and there was nothing about my man to draw any undue attention and other than the fact that he also looked lean and hungry. It was just out of curiosity and because he sat to my immediate right that I took some interest in him. He moved about with an air of what I thought was an artificial politeness. He smiled rather mechanically, I also thought. He had taken down some eight writings on buses that were lined up at the station:

ALLAH IS GREAT
THE LORD IS MY SHEPHERD
ROAD TO HEAVEN
SEEING IS BELIEVING
GOD IS GREAT
FORGIME THEM FATHER
ONE WITH GOD IS MAJORITY
ADAM'S FRUIT
SAVING CHRIST

It was out of this same curiosity that I discovered that the bus for which we had bought the ticket was called *THE LORD IS MY SHEPHERD*. Presently, a small vendor was passing with an almanac entitled *JESUS CONQUERS Satan*. It seemed to interest my man It was in three segments. Segment One portrayed a football match in which Jesus, armed with his cross and a strange football, was proving victorious against a team of black, horned monsters, definitely Satan's cohorts. Segment Two showed a dying man in bed with black horned monsters tearing at him from all sides. The dying man was looking up steadfastly into the sky from which Jesus, Bible in hand, was beckoning him. Segment Three showed Jesus marching on snakes with human heads, on tigers and lions. He was holding up the victory sign.

My man studied the paper very well and bought one which he folded and stored jealously by his side. He next turned to the discotheque man who was playing one church song after the other and remarked:

"You really like Jesus eh?"

"Who?" the boy asked.

"The man whose music you are playing. You like him nnoh?"

"Why not? The man i music de pass market fine fine."

My man scratched his head slightly and I could notice some embarrassment.

"But you must like him," my man said. "Otherwise you won't play his music all the time."

"People like it very much."

"So people like Jesus very much-eh?"

"They buy it for cry-die. Dem like this kind Jesus mizic ova for die place."

My man's countenance changed for a while and then he told the boy: "Give me two cassettes. But I buy them because I love Jesus not because of cry-die."

The boy smiled and said: "Pa if all people be like you I for dong rich. Just buy'am, if you de go throway'am, no problem."

***

Eight, nine, ten, eleven, twelve, thirteen passengers... And then we were ready to move. We chose our seats. My man was sitting almost directly behind the driver. As soon as the driver turned on the engine my man looked round briefly and remarked to the driver:

"I think you like Jesus."

"Why?" the driver asked. "You see cross for my chest?"

"I can see all the signs," my man said, pointing at some three stickers on the inside of the windscreen which read: Christ if the Lion, Satan if the Rat; **All Powers Belong to Jesus; To God Alone my Thanks.**

"Ah ah, pa if thas your reason then na lie. I use all those cheap papers to protect my insurance and vignette from water when they wash the car.. Where I de go with Jesus? You see my like craze man?"

My man looked mortified. Immediately he spoke the words, the driver lit a cigarette and started smoking!

Although we all detested the idea, it was my man who first protested.

"How can you smoke when you have written NO SMOKING in front of you?" he inquired.

"I did not write it," the driver said. "I am secours driver. My friend who owns the car write it."

"But you should respect the rules of the original owner of the car..."

"Ok sa, you win," the driver said, threw the cigarette out of the window and turned on his music at full blast. The song he was playing was a very popular number: *BOBY NA WAN*. My man seemed to be cringing in his seat and, as soon as the record came to an end he gave the driver one of the cassettes he had just bought.

"Is better, sa?"

"Wonderful deliverance," my man said.

The driver turned it on and listened for a minute:

Greater than all is Jesus

Greater than all is his Love for mankind

Jesus the Saviour, Jesus the redeemer...

As if it had been secretly planned, everybody shouted in such loud protest that the driver immediately stopped it and replaced it with another popular number: *MONEY FOR HAND BACK FOR DOWN; AKWARA WOMAN LIKE MONEY.*

Everybody seemed to be enjoying it until my man's neighbour nudged him and complained loudly:

"Pa, if you don't want to listen to this record, don't sing that your *born again* rubbish into my ears!"

My man was not listening. He now sang even louder than the cassette:

I am married to Jesus, Satan leave me alone;

I will praise his name higher and higher until Satan will jump into the abyss;

His name is Jesus, there is no other name but Jesus...

He seemed to have guts, because he was being hushed down from all sides. But the more they shouted, the louder he sang.

"Born again are all hypocrites," somebody shouted.

"Pure Satan," the driver said. "I fight wit dem all the time in this motor. For them only church song..."

"And what's wrong with church songs?" my man asked.

"What's so right in it that you will want everybody to listen only to it? Why should you alone command all of us?" somebody asked.

My man stood his ground. "When the cassette was commanding all of you alone, what did you say?" he inquired.

"It disturbed nobody," I said, and then asking the driver to lower the music somehow, I asked him: "Are you the only one who knows God? Are you the only one who has read the bible?"

"Some read the Bible, but without comprehension! Such people do not know that the Bible contains the mind of God, the state of man, the way of salvation, the doom of sinners like you, and the happiness of believers like me. You must be grateful to God who has created you. You must be thankful to Him, for as John 3 says in verses 16 and 17 say: For God so loved the world that he sent his only begotten son, that whosoever believeth in him should not perish, but have everlasting life...." he went on.

My man had virtually opened a can of worms!

"You don't go to church, Pa Jesus?" somebody asked mockingly.

"I am not Jesus. Nobody...," he protested sharply.

"Mr Judas...."

"You may call me names, but I know who I am. I am Dennis Nunqam Ndendemajem, a believer in God...."

"Okay Mr Jejemejem or whatever you call yourself, do you not go to church?"

"Of course I go..."

"Such people even sleep in church," somebody else put in.

"What if I go to church?" my man resumed.

"That's where you thank God," the man said, "not in the midst of people. That's hypocrisy..."

"If you are truly grateful then you will thank God everywhere, every time, every waking hour of your life. You should never stop thanking him because he can never stop loving you."

"So because God has done you a service he should not rest, he should not attend to anybody else? Minute minute, you are behind him, 'Thank you papa, for the thing wey you been do,' God is in the latrine, you are behind him with prayer! God wants to eat, you are behind him with thank you prayer! God wants to help some other person, you say he should only listen to you. Don't you see that you make a nuisance of yourself before God and man?"

"God is almighty and has no need of our human functions, he has no need of sleep, no need of rest, no need of food..."

"Even if he did, gentleman, he would not, precisely because of mosquitoes like you making noise in his ears every second. There's no other way of pleasing God than ceaseless prayer?"

"Of course there are others!"

"Ah those noises you make at midnight over people's homes?"

"Those are not meaningless noises. We awaken people from the slumber of sin to the awareness of the existence of God. In fact I am down here to do just that for Mbongo."

"I don't think you have anything doing."

"Working for God is work enough, anything else that you do is without meaning because it does not guarantee you salvation."

"Do you have a family?

"I have a family."

"How do you feed them? With the scriptures and crusades or something?"

My man took off at a tangent: "Be not ashamed of the testimony of our Lord, nor me his prisoner, Second Timothy verse 8 tells us, but be thou partaker of the afflictions of the gospel according to the power of God." He immediately jumped into another irritating song, to the chagrin of everybody:

Some people de ask me say, weti de make you fine?
I just answer them say, na Jesus de make me fine
I de fine, I de fine, I de fine
I de fine, I de fine, fine, fine;

The passengers waited until he took in his breath and then they all fell on him:

"Look at somebody who thinks he is fine," somebody said. "What's the difference between you and a scarecrow? Go and look at yourself in a mirror."

"Can he have a mirror?" another asked.

"Say what you like," my man said. "Christ is my mirror. Father forgive them for they know not what they do. I am covered by the blood of Jesus who died on the cross to save us from sin."

I couldn't stand him any longer. I thought I should call him to order. "Who told you that Jesus died to save us from sin?" I asked..

"It is written in the Holy Book..."

"Jesus died to pay for the sins and crimes of his family, his forefathers! If you follow the story of his background you will wonder why they did not even hand him upside down." I told him. "Quote me anywhere," I told him. "My name is Ticha Domenique, I am H.M. and I teach scriptures. I have been teaching it for fifteen years, and I know the in and out of the Bible. Jesus was the offspring of David, was he not?"

"Your own lips have said it," my man said. "Who says he wasn't?"

"Good, do you recall that David seized the wife of Uriah, a soldier and then caused the man to be killed at the battle front so that he took the man's wife?"

My man was silent.

"Jesus was the offspring of Abraham, the Abraham who almost gave his son to *menyongo,* if God's eyes were not sharp...Jesus was the offspring of Jacob, the Jacob same who stole his friend's birth right by disguising as the brother to his blind father!"

My man was silent.

"Jesus was the offspring of Kain, the first murderer who killed his brother ,Abel! Jesus was the offspring of Adam and Eve, the first couple to steal from God. And when they hang such a man for the crimes of his parents you say he died to save us. That you are covered by the blood of Jesus. Why are you not covered by his piss?"

"Or by his shit even," somebody cut in. There was a loud derisive laugh and I could see that my man was lost.

"Look at his immediate parentage," I said.. He is the product of an adulterous relationship: his mother was impregnated when she was still the legally married wife of Joseph...."

My man took refuge in another song:

He is a miracle working God

He is a miracle working God...

I was still on his back! "How many miracles did Jesus perform?" I asked him.

"Many," my man said lamely. "He made the blind to see, the lame to walk, the deaf to hear, the dumb to talk. He raised the dead from the dead. He performed countless miracles..."

"There again you are deceiving yourself. Achievement can only be established in terms of figures. Your Jesus made one blind person to see. If you consider how many blind people were in Israel at the time, how many lame, how many deaf and the like, you will see that he did not even scratch the surface of the problems. You say he raised the dead. How many people died on the day Lazarus died? Why did he raise only Lazarus and not the others too? Were they all not children of God? He was a *fayman!* Look at what he did to prove his greatness: he took madness out of a man and put into a herd of pigs! Those were somebody's pigs, and he did so without permission and without compensation. When he was entering Jerusalem, he did not buy an ass. He simple took it from its owner. He was capitalising on the fact that the people were ignorant. If it were these days, he would pay dearly for it...

Chapter Twenty

Dennis Nunqam Nedendemajem

GOD ANSWERED my prayers and freed me from the claws of those devils, from the world of sin! I had seen for myself, first hand, the magnitude of the work which Our Father had in hand to reconquer God's lost territory because Satan was all over the place.

I arrived Mbongo at 11 o'clock in the morning precisely. From the park I walked the two kilometres distance to the Government Primary School where my two children were registered. I arrived the school compound not too long after they had returned from long break and were just trying to settle down. I went straight to the Head Master's office. The man whom people generally called Pa Bosco was probably in his sixties and would under normal circumstances have been long retired.

He had been taken over from the private sector into the government service and so his age of retirement was fixed as from the day he was taken over. It was more than likely that he would be there for twenty more years. He was dark, of medium height, and very heavily built. His head was bald and one cold see the ceaseless efforts he had made to conceal the whiteness of his hair. In spite of the line of dye which ran even into the areas where there was no hair, there were stray patches of white, grey and even brown especially to the back.

He was wearing heavily rimmed spectacles with scratched lenses through which one wondered how he ever saw anything, over dull-looking eyes below which the skin fell in folds. He had a thick whitish-grey moustache which he had tried very unsuccessfully to paint black. He was a great snuff taker, and there was much evidence that he had taken some not too long ago for he held a brown handkerchief in his left hand which he used for cleaning his nostrils as he spoke.

"Good morning, HM," I greeted politely.

The man cleaned his nostril, looked over his spectacles and bellowed in a deep heavy voice:

"Morning. Welcome."

"Praise the Lord," I said and then tried to introduce myself.

"I know you, very well," Bosco said. "You are not the man who abandoned his wife and children?"

I smiled dryly, stammered and then sat back in silence.

"What can I do for you?" Bosco inquired.

"I have my two children here, Dieudonne and Felix Ndendemajem," I told him.

"Since when?" Pa Bosco asked aggressively.

"Since they were admitted here. One, Dieudonne was admitted three years ago. Felix was admitted, I think, year before last."

The Head Master reflected for a while and, tapping a ruler on the books in front of him asked:

"When did you last see these children you call yours?"

I tightened my lips, bit my lower lip and said: "Fourteen months."

The man put down the ruler he was holding, pulled off his spectacles which he placed on the register in front of him and, folding his hands, sat back and inquired: "Is that normal, Mr. Dennis?"

I could feel my eyes blink several times.

The man continued: "Is it normal for a parent to abandon his own children for years without any just cause?"

My right hand went to my head and I scratched it briefly. The Lord sent me a word and I quoted Matthew 7:1-2: "HM," I said "*Judge not that ye be not judged. For with what judgement you judge, you will be judged; and with the measure that you use, it will be measured back to you.* I came here to see them."

Pa Bosco sneered to himself and looked into my eyes as though he was talking with somebody who had taken leave of his senses.

"You cannot see those children in this school, Mr. Dennis," he said.

"Why?" I asked.

"The mother of these children, her parents, and a respectable doctor have given instructions that you should on no account be permitted to have access to those children."

"I have come to see those children," I said. "I have to see them before I leave."

"Before you leave?" the man asked with more surprise.

***

Pa Bosco sent a teacher to fetch the two boys. As soon as they came into the office and saw me they both screamed in horror until the teacher who had brought them led them back out.

Bosco and myself looked at each other fixedly. Finally he asked:

"Were those not the children you call yours, Mr. Dennis?"

"They were," I admitted.

"Is that how children react to the presence of their parents?"

"No."

"Then how do you explain all this strange behaviour?"

"The reason is simple," I told him. I could clearly see that he was still in the dark. "Somebody like my wife or the relatives, or the doctor of respect you talked of, has caused my children to behave the way they did," I said. "That is wrong. That is sin for First John chapter 5 verse 17 tells us that *"All wrong doing is sin.* And James 4, verse 17 says *"Anyone who knows the good he ought to do and doesn't do it, sins."*

"So, sir, your sin begins only when children turn their back on their parents, not when their parent abandons them?" he asked. I could see the devil in him, urging him to sin, and to use bad language.

I did not answer. Instead I opened my bag and took out two small books of Bible Stories For Children.

"Give them these when I am gone," I entreated Pa Bosco.

"That is not what I do," he told me.

I smiled and walked away. What he had just done did not bother me one bit!

***

I decided I would go to Manda as scheduled and know why she had misled the children to that extent. I think one of the teachers went ahead of me and by the time I arrived Sabongari where my house was everybody seemed to know I was on my way there.

From about 200 metres away I could see the window and door of my house open. But when I came closer and looked up they were both shut. My former neighbours and relatives stood in their verandas and doorsteps watching me in something like wrath as I passed. I made an effort to greet everybody, but none responded. Not even big mammy, the old woman in whom I confided so often in the past. I walked up undaunted to the door of my house and knocked. It was locked from inside.

"Manda! Manda!" I called.

There was no answer. I turned round and walked across the compound up to the old woman.

"I greeted you, mama, but you did not answer," I said to her, "even though you heard me. I greeted the other neighbours down the quarter, but they all just stood looking at me pass. I am just from school where I tried to talk to my children, but they screamed as if I have become a ghost or some wild animal. I saw my window and door open from the distance, but as I came nearer they were shut. The door is locked from inside, meaning that Manda is inside. I have knocked and called and called but she would not respond. I want to know what is happening. Mama, please tell me. Who is this person causing all my people to sin and fall short of the glory of God?"

There was a very long silence which seemed to imply that the old woman did not actually want to say anything. Finally she began:

"My child Dennis, the way you talk, you make it look like the people are wrong and you are right. You make it look like nothing wrong has happened between you and your family. My child Dennis, are you still the same person we once knew in this quarter?"

I was silent. "If I am different," I said to myself, "it is because I have seen the light and because I am married to Jesus."

"My child Dennis," she went on, "have you ever seen where a man would put a child in his wife's stomach and then leave them all for five years without any reason? What do you think they have been eating? What do you think they have been wearing?"

"Matthew 6, 25," I said to myself and then said aloud *"Do not worry about your life, what you will eat or what you will drink; nor about your body, what you will put on. Is not life more than food and the body more than clothing?"*

The old woman rose and entered into her house and shut the door.

***

It was only on this trip that I noticed how people were taking my involvement in ALCA. I left a Bible and two small **Bible Story Books For Children** at the door into my house and went back away without seeing Manda, my wife. I had mapped out a busy schedule for my journey which I had to follow very strictly. Having failed to talk either to Manda or the children the next item on the programme was a visit to the Mbongo Urban Council.

There I was to deliver a letter from Reverend Pastor Shrapnell applying to use the municipal stadium for the impending Crusade. The devil seemed to have gone ahead of me again, for the Delegate of the Mbongo Urban Council read the letter and told me:

"If you are wise, don't set your feet on this soil, even if you will pay a million francs. What you have done to your wife and children because of that your church is such an embarrassment to everybody. So long as I remain delegate for this urban council, that religion will never be permitted to set foot here."

So saying he rose, I too rose with him and then the man locked his office and drove away. I left a Bible with his secretary to give him and then left Mbongo for Ovenga. It was part of my plan to visit Elken Moore, if he was still there and if he could still recognise me.

Chapter Twenty-One

Elken Moore

In this bloodyfucking sonafobitch-of-a-diplomat, you have to draw up your weekly programme buddy, otherwise these niggars will suck the hell out of you. They would want everything for just nothing. I usually got out of bed at 7.30 every morning, took my breakfast at 8 o'clock, and went to work at 9.

They must have been something like 10 blokes waiting to see me. I went through the visitors' book and then shut it.

"Let them come in the order of filling the form," I instructed my secretary. I must have lost my memory when the bloke came in and stood in front of me and introduced himself.

"Doesn't ring a bell," I said.

"Dennis Nunqam Ndendemajem the artist," he repeated.

My right palm rose to my forehead and struck it twice.

"Doesn't still ring a bell," I said.

There was a silence and then Dennis said:

"I had an exposition here some seven years ago. I was even given a government scholarship to study art in America, but it all ended up in smoke because of some kind of politics. A friend of mine, Dr. Maximillian Essemo came here seventeen months ago to arrange for an exposition..."

I could feel my expression change suddenly. I smiled to him as my habit was, and told him:

"Of course I know you. I remember the good doctor who came here last year to talk on your behalf. Age is creeping fast on me," I confessed. An inexplicable overture of friendliness had suddenly entered my voice. I had been smoking my cigar, and why not? I returned the cigar to my lips and, placing my right hand on Dennis' shoulder showed him where to sit.

Once comfortably seated he told me how after temporarily abandoning art he had resumed it at The Salvation Colony where he had already made 46 paintings including several murals for the halls and ALCA churches across the province and the world over. He had come to ask for permission to mount an exposition in the near future.

"Of course," I beamed. "You know what?" I asked.

He looked at me rather quizzically, but with subdued excitement. "We continue to hold you in very high esteem," I told him, and I actually meant what I said. I could see his eyes open with pride. "I told your doctor friend when he was here last year that I had taken a particular liking to your works. I told him how much we did to encourage you. But, as you know, we only make suggestions and leave to your government to implement... I show the film of your vernissage every time we have a great occasion involving aspiring artists."

My artist friend seemed to smile faintly. I asked him to wait outside until I had attended to the last visitor. I took him into an inner room where we usually relay the news from Washington. I sorted out his video cassette, mounted the equipment and called on Dennis to see himself and his works ten years ago.

Throughout the show which lasted fifty minutes, Dennis looked on in a serene contemplative silence. He did not react to the running commentary I made all along. At the end I summed it up with a challenge:

"How can you beat that?"

"I can beat it," he said confidently, defiantly.

"I'd be glad to see you do it," I said. "I'd be glad to help. Where are you from right now?" I asked.

"I spent the night at PYC, the Presbyterian Youth Centre," he said, "coming from Mbongo."

"And during the intervening years, where have you been, what have you been doing?" I asked, "especially since your friend contacted me."

He took his time and said: "Since I lost that scholarship darkness enfolded my life and I could not get myself to do anything. Now that I have found another fellowship in Jesus, I can see clearly. Before, I shut my door and my life to God. Now that I have seen the light, I can do just about anything..."

"I happen to be an atheist," I said. I hate niggars trying to preach the Bible to me! That response seemed to have injected a small dose of poison into a conversation so well begun.

"Light, darkness or shade are elements of art which you handled so well in the past," I told him. "Just let us know when you are ready. About how many paintings do you have?"

"From here I go to Menako where I expect about a dozen or so at Dr. Essemo's place where I lived. I have some in Mbongo which I shall try to have sent to me in The Colony. In all I might have some sixty pieces."

"Did you say the colony?" I inquired.

"The Colony, Sir," he said. "Salvation Colony."

I said nothing else. I had been asked numerous questions about Salvation Colony, most of whom I have been unable to answer. If the African allows himself to be deceived, he has himself to blame.

***

An idea struck me.

"I'll try something," I told Dennis. "I'll give Dr. Essemo a surprise call." I searched my address book for the address and then telephoned Menako immediately.

Dr. Essemo received the call personally in his office.

"I sure remember you," Dr. Essemo said after I introduced myself and was wondering whether he still recognised me. "How can I forget. I came there some time ago last year to solicit your help on behalf of a neurotic friend of mine..."

"You are talking of Mr. Dennis Nunqam, I suppose?" I inquired.

"Yes," he said. "I am sorry I put you through all that trouble. The arse hole preferred to hang himself..."

"What?" I was shocked.

"Mr. Dennis Nunqam Ndendemajem, the devil I did everything to help out of his crushing poverty. He hanged himself."

"Wer-e-menet," I said. I looked across at Dennis. He was certainly following Dr. Essemo's loud angry voice. I am not the superstitious type, but, for a while I feared I might have been talking to a ghost, not the Dennis I once knew. "We may not be talking about the same person..."

"Sure we are," Dr. Essemo said.

"But Dennis is alive," I said. "And the reason I am phoning is because he was here. He planned to see you later today. Actually he has put in a request to mount an art exposition. He said he was coming to see you concerning some dozen or so paintings and sketches he left in your keeping."

"He must be kidding. It sounds strange, Mr. Moore."

"Why strange?"

"Because that cow will do nothing we think can make his hopeless life meaningful."

"Did you say he hanged himself?" I asked.

"He did. He was saved only by a miracle."

"You are now talking," I felt relieved. "When I spoke to him he looked very alright to me," I said.

"He may be still breathing," Dr. Essemo said. "But he is a corpse just awaiting burial, as far as I know. Did he say he left paintings with me?"

"Ya," I nodded. "At least he gave me that impression."

"He must be dreaming," Dr. Essemo said. "Mr. Moore," he called again.

"You are on," I said.

"Let me be frank with you, since the monster has come to you. When the arsehole failed to bring discredit to my house by attempting to hang himself here, I chased him away and burned everything that could ever remind me of him."

"Burned them?"

"Yes. I had no choice. By the way, did he have the courage to tell you all that I tried to do for him and how he tried to pay me back?"

Dr. Essemo's bitterness caused a certain discomfort in my veins.

"The American Cultural Affairs Office is not a consultancy, Dr. Essemo," I said. "When you came here I told you I liked his works. You promised to bring him back into the limelight. I never heard from you again. He has showed up to express the desire to do what you wanted to do for him. Why would I want to know more than that?"

The niggar hung up on me. The son of a bitch indeed! I took in a very long breath and then shaking off the embarrassment I turned to Dennis.

"Did you try to hang yourself, Mr. Nunqam?" I asked.

"I did, Mr. Moore," he admitted honestly. "And had he not chased me from his house I would have really done it someday."

"Why would you do that?" He put his hands together, leaned towards me and began softly:

"I had no choice. I was married with my children, and was working, though on small pay. My friend did not think that a poor man could think for himself. He believed that the rich man alone can think and act for the poor man. I don't know how to put it, but his goodness killed me. I became a prisoner of his generosity. It made me look meaningless in front of every single human being. I saw no future for myself. It was all total darkness. And now that I am talking to you, I am not allowed to see my children or my wife. Because he has convinced the whole world that I am mad, since I did not do his will. Do I look like a mad man, Mr. Moore?"

In spite of myself I smiled and glanced at my watch. He was taking far too much of my time.

"Not to the best of my knowledge," I told him.

"I have pardoned them all," he added unnecessarily. "That is all behind me now. I cannot think of doing so any more. I have found the light."

Chapter Twenty-Two

Dr. Maximillian Essemo Aleukwinchaa

Like a spectre from the past Dennis showed up at my gate some four hours after I spoke to that stupid American. It must have been three in the afternoon or something of the sort. When I heard the gate bell I pulled the curtain to one side and looked out. I watched him lean towards the gate for a while and ask my boy:

"Do you know me, brother?"

"Who you call ya brother?" Amos my yard boy asked insolently. I was glad he recognised Dennis, and also that he had not yet forgotten the instructions I once gave all of them.

"You know me?" he asked again.

"Were you not the one who hanged behind the house there?" Amos inquired off-handedly.

I could see a gentle smile on Dennis' lips. A smile indeed!

"Who said I hanged?" he asked.

"Were we not the people who removed you from the ground?" Amos asked him, which made me smile.

"Do people hang on the ground?" he asked.

"But you come for what?" the man asked.

"Is Dr. Essemo in?"

"Who wants him?"

"I want him," he said.

Amos looked Dennis up and down and walked away when Dennis repeated the request.

"People don't enter this compound?" he asked.

"Is that what I said?" the yard boy asked.

"They say we should not open the gate for people like you. They say we should never allow you to set foot here."

"I want to come in there. I want to talk to Dr. Essemo," he said. I could not continue to play hide and seek with a ragamuffin. I decided to come out and tell him a piece of my mind, once and for all.

I met Amos on the stairs as he was coming to talk to me. Dennis had gone back and sat on the cement embankment at the entrance.

"Good afternoon, Dr. Essemo," he greeted as soon as he saw me downstairs.

"What have you come to do here?" I asked.

"To see you, Doctor," the idiot said.

"Am I a cinema?"

"No, Doctor," he responded in his usual offensive politeness, rising and coming closer to the gate.

"Why do you want to see me?" I inquired. The fury was obvious in my tone.

"Many things, Doctor."

"Talk from there," I declared, walked down and towards the gate. "Mr. Dennis," I began, "I hope some sense has finally come into your head."

He seemed to smile briefly and then he said firmly:

"Sense has always been in my head, Dr. Essemo..."

"Sense has always been in your head and then you behave like a pig?" I asked.

"How did I behave like a pig, Dr. Essemo?" the swine asked.

"Put food in a plate and give to a pig. It will first throw the food on the ground and rub it with mud..."

"Man shall not live by bread alone, Dr. Essemo," he said like a Jehovah Witness, "but out of any word that comes out of the mouth of God."

I looked at him with total derision.

"What exactly has brought you here?" I asked.

"I lived in the dark, Dr. Essemo," he began again. "I have now seen the light, the light of Jesus..."

"So what have you come to do here now that you have the light?"

"To show you the light I have seen, Dr. Essemo," he said. "To show the light of God. For it is written, Dr. Essemo, no man lighteth a lamp and putteth it under a bushel but on..."

I clapped my hands in utter amazement. My eyes watering with mirth I personally opened the gate and beckoned to him and showed him where to sit on a chair in the veranda downstairs.

I then hurried back up to the parlour and immediately telephoned my friend, Willie.

"Guess who is here," I said to Willie.

"I cannot," the man said.

"Mr. Dennis Nunqam Ndendemajem himself is here."

"No kidding. The hanging man?"

"Himself," I said.

"What has he come to do? Don't allow him to go near a rope or a tree branch."

We both laughed for a moment and then I asked:

"Do you know what he has come to do?"

"Can't guess."

"He has come to show me the light."

"Which light? Is he working for the Electricity Corporation now?" Willie, the same old stick in the mud, with his usual humour!

"You better come and ask him yourself."

***

Willie did not come until an hour later. Throughout that period I remained in my room listening to my afternoon news. Dennis, the man of light, sat there reading his bible. As soon as my friend horned at the gate I came out and descended to meet him.

Dennis rose with a strange smile and greeted him with the same politeness that he had greeted me.

"Good afternoon, Mr. Dennis," Willie answered, shook Dennis' hand briskly and immediately remarked:

"Doc, do you notice a phenomenal change in this fellow? See the radiance in his eyes." He then turned to Dennis and inquired: "What have you been doing to yourself that you are looking so good, so high spirited?"

"Who gives a damn?" I asked.

"I hear you work now for the Electricity Corporation," Willie resumed in his customary comic manner.

"I work for God," Dennis said. "I do not work for the Electricity Corporation," he said unsmiling.

"But they say you give light..."

"Yes, I show the light," he admitted, and then quoted the same biblical text that he had quoted to me.

"Holy Moses," Willie exclaimed. "How is your family?" he changed the topic.

"Well," Dennis replied.

"Shit," I cursed. "Why can't you be honest, Mr. Pope Dennis? You answer for a family you have not seen for years..."

"Then where has he been all this while?" Willie asked.

"Ask the cow," I said.

The man turned towards Dennis again.

"Salvation Colony," he said. "We live there..."

"In that devilish place?"

"It is the house of God," Dennis told him resolutely.

"You live there with your family?"

Dennis admitted.

"Another stupid lie," I cut in. "His miserable family is abandoned in Mbongo."

He smiled and turned to Willie. "All God's children are one family..."

"You are just around here and you would not stop by?" Willie asked. He seemed to take Dennis more seriously than myself. "What has brought you here? The light?"

Dennis nodded.

"You will never know how far you could have gone just living here and doing what was expected of you..."

"I could not have gone far, Dr. Essemo, I went as far as I could have gone..."

"Of course you couldn't have, you were too idiotic."

"Not that, Dr. Essemo."

"Then what? You have any idea of what it means to be a doctor?"

"I know, Dr. Essemo."

"What do you know about being doctor?"

"I know that he is somebody who takes care of the sick and suffering..."

"And you do not think even that is doing a lot?"

"I think it is, Dr. Essemo," he said and then went on to annoy me all the more. "But when you first talked about the medical profession to me two years ago, you made me see that being a doctor simply means swimming in money, riding a Mercedes, building skyscrapers..."

There was an abrupt silence in which I felt a slight sense of guilt. The cow would make me feel guilty?

"And that is why, Dr. Essemo, in First Timothy Chapter 6 verses 6 to 9, we are told that *'We brought nothing into this world,"* he continued, *"and it is certain we can carry nothing out.*

"But those who desire to be rich fall into temptation and a snare, and into many foolish and harmful lusts which drown men in destruction and perdition."

"Leave that rubbish," I shouted. "You got it all wrong, Dennis," I said softly but uneasily. "Being a doctor is a good job and being in a good job means being rich. In the same way, you cannot live a rich life without driving a good car or living in a comfortable house...

"It is written, Dr. Essemo..."

"You are getting on my nerves once more. Tell me, for the last time, why have you come? To show me how you couldn't read for a single paper in the GCE but you can now recite the whole bible?"

"Yes," Dennis said with irritating calmness. "I have also come to collect my paintings..."

"You have finally decided to paint?" Willie asked with keenest interest.

"Yes, Doctor," he said.

Willie once more drew attention to what he described as the idiot's poise, the air confidence with which he made his point. "Our man may actually have seen some kind of light, you know? Look at this Mr. Dennis who never looked anybody in the face, who never looked up, he is all full of poise and confidence."

"I give a damn," I said. "Let him tell me what he came here for and get the hell out of here." In my mind I had prepared an answer, should the swine ask me anything concerning Manda's new baby. I was yet to learn of Gertrude's presence in the Colony! "You were so dazed that you slept with your own wife without knowing it?" I had planned to ask him and then send him away.

But he said nothing about the new baby.

"I have also come to collect my manuscripts which I left here," he said. "You see, Doctor William, I lived here as if I was in a trance. It is interesting to see what you do in a trance. Since I wrote many things here and made many drawings, I thought it would be good for me to see what I used to draw or write while in that state of mind...."

"Wonders shall never end," Willie said, looking at Dennis with a mixture of disbelief and what I thought appeared to be admiration.

"A cow which could not wipe his nose," I began, "coming to show me the light, to talk to me about God's grace. You must be sick in the head. If I did not possess God's grace, how could I have gotten what I had to the extent of inviting you to come and live with me?

"Look at me, Dennis," I said with priggish pride. "And look at yourself. Compare and tell me which of us can talk of God's grace, or about the greatness of God."

I know what I looked like. I stood a very well-cut figure of close to two metres in height. I was wearing a charcoal grey suit over a pink shirt that I had not worn before. A gold wrist chain dangled from my left wrist. I was naturally fairer in complexion than Dennis, but the extra care I took of my body made me look even lighter. My palms, for example, were extremely white and baby-like.

The hair on my head was thick but well-kept, so was my moustache which was linked to my low beard with a thin line of hair that looked almost artificial in the mirror. I was wearing a pair of sunglasses, the golden frame of which contrasted conspicuously with the background of my dark brows and side burns which descended to just below my ears.

I threw a casual glance at the man who had come to talk to me about God! My lips twisted in a smile of obvious contempt, and I looked away. Only a man of his disposition could have failed to see that of the two of us I looked more like one who had benefited from God's grace and one, therefore, who was better placed to talk about the greatness of God.

"It is written, Dr. Essemo," he began very calmly, determined to have his way, "the Gospel according to St John Chapter 2 verses 15 and 16; *do not love the world or the things in the world. If anyone loves the world, the love of the Father is not in him.*

For all that is in the world - the lust of the flesh, the lust of the eyes, and the pride of life - is not of the Father but is of the world..."

"Vomit the whole bible here, vomit the Koran," I spat. "The bottom line is that I have burnt all those things you are talking about. And if you do not leave this compound within the next five minutes, Dennis, I shall burn you to ashes the way I burned that your rubbish, and let me tell you that nothing will happen to me."

He smiled, ignored my threat and rage, and looked at Willie.

"You may be on top of life, but that is because you were born there, Dr. Essemo," the idiot gave me the credit I deserved with sullen persistence. "That is because you were born there. You gave me only what you had - riches. If you had the light you would have given me, or helped me to see God's grace, not earthly glories.

"Matthew 10, verse 26 says *Do not fear those who kill the body but cannot kill the soul. But rather fear Him who is able to destroy both soul and body in hell.*"

I rose, pulled the ass by the sleeves the way I remembered doing about a year ago, took him to the gate and, opening it said:

"I see you here again, I shall shoot and bury you. That should tell you how much of God's grace I have already."

Part Two

So oft it chances in particular men,
That for some vicious mole of nature in them,
As in their birth, wherein they are not guilty
(Since nature cannot choose his origin),
By the o'ergrowth of some complexion,
Oft breaking down the pales and forts of reason,
Or by some habit that too much o'er-leavens
The form of plausive manners - that these men,
Carrying, I say, the stamp of one defect,
Being nature's livery or fortune's star,
His virtues else, be they as pure as grace,
As infinite as man may undergo,
Shall in the general censure take corruption
From that particular fault. The dram of evil
Doth all the noble substance often doubt
To his own scandal.

[*Shakespeare: Hamlet*]

Chapter Twenty-Three

Istromo Ngiawa: Master Planner

A journalist who starves is a journalist who has never learned his trade. Yes, that was what I told my man, Cosmas. No way we would spend so many years in Nigeria, see how much money journalists make just by using their wits, just by putting their finger on the right commodity, and then die of hunger. "If the government will not employ us" I told him, "let us employ ourselves." I told him we should create a newspaper like no other, one which would handle topics of great interest to the public such as raw sex and crime, anything scandalous. My man bought the idea, and so was born THE NAKED TRUTH. It was Cosmas who suggested the title of the paper. We both liked the name. My own contribution was the motto: BRINGING THE UNSEEN TO THE EYES OF THE UNSEEING.

Ridiculing ALCA or Shrapnell was never the goal of our paper from the start. ALCA only became important to us when Cosmas thought we could use the paper to defame Shrapnell and so cause his moyo to become disappointed with it and abandon it. It was in this context that we began to dig out scandals relating to sects. Thereafter, ALCA became the focus of our attention.

Cosmas himself had been a member of the DO ME I DO YOU church of Calabar in Nigeria. From his experience and the way they were usually ridiculed, he knew that it was easy to associate a sect with any sort of scandal and the public would believe it. At the time, as far as ALCA was concerned, we did not know exactly what it was we were looking for, but Cosmas was confident that there must be some unpalatable truth about ALCA that could sell the paper. It may be the relationship between the leaders and people's wives, daughters, the widows, divorcees, and the blind but beautiful women who swelled the numbers of converts. Just anything.

***

We sat down and drew our strategy, and on September 18th 1972, Cosmas and myself visited Salvation Colony, sworn to discover a scandal or superimpose one.

"We are freelance journalists," we began when Shrapnell agreed to talk to us. "What we have heard about this place is phenomenal," Cosmas told him. "We are about to launch a bi-weekly newspaper - THE NAKED TRUTH - and we think it would boost the image and popularity of the Colony if we gave it extensive coverage in the maiden issue. I even have my brother-in-law here, Mr. Dennis Nunqam. He has spoken so well of your activities."

Shrapnell felt flattered, as we had suspected he would. He personally showed us round the entire Colony. We took pictures and even spoke to moyo Dennis before returning to Shrapnell's office where we said we had a few personal questions to ask him.

"Why Salvation Colony?" I inquired.

"Salvation means several things," Shrapnell told us.

"First of all it means deliverance from evil, evil of every kind, within and without , now and to come. Secondly, it refers to the gaining of good, the life with God and all that this brings. Finally it means the help of God. In a word, salvation is deliverance and life by the help of God... *You did he make alive,*' St. Paul writes. *That is salvation, being alive to God and to every good which God's world can bring you,*" he concluded.

"Is it true that you make the blind see and the lame walk?" I went on.

"Thy own lips have said it," Shrapnell said with a touch of humour and vanity. Then he ran his hand under his clean-shaven chin and began a bit more seriously: "Not in an obvious and physical sense, no. I bring light to the blind in the sense that I make them understand their predicament in a different light. For instance, I make them see that even in that eyeless state, theirs is not the end of the world, that they have direct access to God, that they can achieve a lot, even more than many with eyes. I do the same for the lame. I make them rise above their disabilities into greater heights..."

"The general atmosphere here has been described as one of total happiness, would you agree?"

"I should think so," Shrapnell replied. "People would not continue to come here in these numbers if there was doubt that they were going to find happiness."

"What would you think is the secret to this attainment? Would you think it is the Soul to Soul programme so many people talk about?" I asked.

"I would think you have hit the nail on the head. I have spent many years studying human nature, and I have to conclude that pain is invariably mitigated when victims share their experiences, and also when people with different types of handicaps live together. As the human mind is apt to compare things, a person with a particular handicap usually tends to think he is worse or better off than another. The blind man who can walk, for instance, thinks he is better than the lame man who has all his eyes but cannot walk.

"In the same way, the woman who is bitter and pained by the fact that she has lost all her three, four or five children, feels she is better than the barren woman. The reverse is also true. Thus, in the organization of the living structure of Salvation Colony, I made sure that the lame and the blind lived together and shared the same recreational facilities, the barren women lived with those who had lost all their children, the deaf and dumb live with the albinos, the women with abnormally large breasts which may have caused them to be neglected by society, live in the vicinity of those who have nothing to show for their womanhood by way of breasts, divorcees live with widows...."

"There is also this **Heart to Heart** Programme, Pastor," I said, "what is it, and how does it help your followers? How does it fit into the scheme of things?"

After a very long hesitation which Cosmas noted in his book he said dismissively:

"It is what it is, bringing hearts together..."

We were careful not to jeopardise the interview. I nudged Cosmas with the elbow and he went to something else.

"On the whole about how many people do you have in here?" he asked.

"About a hundred. There are sixteen albinos, eleven widows, five barren women, thirteen blind, nine lame, six heavy-breasted, five non-breasts, four former prostitutes, five dwarfs and seven jailbirds, a good number of beggars."

Cosmas' eyes met mine and he raised a brow. Cosmas inquired:

"But why only the bizarre? Why this preoccupation with monstrosities?"

"They are not monstrosities as such," Shrapnell said. "It is because society tends to look on them from that ridiculous standpoint that we bring them here, for as Jesus said, I come not to seek the righteous but sinners to repentance... Problem is that since these our brethren look a little different from others, the tendency is for the rest of mankind to treat them with disdain, as though they are subhuman...

"Every form of existence is an expression of God's infinite nature," he broke into a brief but well-conned sermon, " a spark of the Divine, struck off on the anvil of creation, given life and identity in our Father... The blind, the lame, the hungry, the well-fed, dwarf, the giant, are all forms in which God manifests his infinity. To despise any one of these is to despise God. Multiplicity of man indicates multiplicity of God. God himself is infinite. And so, man, created in his own image, must be infinite.... Every single creature represents God in some form or other."

Cosmas took down notes.

"So you do not find anything wrong in an albino, a dwarf, a cripple or a blind man, pastor" he inquired.

"I say whatever way we look at them, we must not lose face of the fact that they express in their various natures God's infinity."

"About how much ground does this colony occupy?"

"Two acres or so."

"How do you raise money to institute such a mammoth project? I guess it must have cost you a fortune."

"Not so much of a fortune. Much of the land was donated by brethren."

"The rest was paid for by ACCA, the American Council of Churches in Africa and other donor organizations. We are constantly in touch with each other. We are on their mailing list. We keep them informed of our activities and needs..."

Cosmas took down some notes again.

"Why do you need this information, if I may ask?" Shrapnell asked. It was me who responded:

"As a journalist and the editor of a young paper like THE NAKED TRUTH, I am anxious to feed the public with new news. Have you been interviewed before?"

"Several times."

"By newspaper editors?"

"Generally it is the radio and television."

"That's why I think anything from here would be newsworthy."

"Why don't you come sometime? I am rather busy."

"Why not, I can come any other time. After all the place

is not running away. Just that having made a start, if I allow some other journalist to cover the event I shall have lost."

I sensed that Shrapnell was getting uncomfortable with the searching nature of the questions.

"One last question before we part," I said. "Are you married? If so are you living here with your wife? If not, do you not miss your wife, living among so many women?"

"No man having put his hand on the plough and looking back is fit for the kingdom of heaven," Shrapnell said and refused to answer any further questions. We had had all that we wanted. We did not need to quote him verbatim. It was enough that he had granted us the interview. We could then concoct anything we needed and use the way we want.

Chapter Twenty-Four

Cosmas Mfetebeunu

We worked ceaselessly and by the 9th of October the maiden issue of **THE NAKED TRUTH** appeared on the newspaper stands. There were three scandals: the first concerned a university lecturer who was caught making love to a student on the desk in his office, having forgotten to lock the door. The second concerned a highly-placed lady who had cut open her own thigh and transported cocaine in it to America by having a doctor friend of hers stitch it up again.

However, we had our eyes mainly on ALCA! As we had planned, Salvation Colony occupied the two centre pages. There was a large picture of Shrapnell on the top right hand corner. Below the picture was that of THE BRETHREN'S KEEPERS, Shrapnell's twelve close collaborators including Dennis whom the man had chosen his second-in-command.

We took time to make the article as thorough as possible. We began most harmlessly, saying everything that needed to be known about The Colony. And then very deliberately we added much that did not need to be known, and which was sure to draw attention to it. We appended a sketch map of the place showing in a very painstaking manner every location in relation to the other. The paper ended with the call on the public to react to the information in the next issue.

There was also a **VOX POP** page on crucial topics in each issue. If nobody said anything we were determined to tickle them into saying something about ALCA. Fortunately for us, the public reacted just as we had predicted. The **VOX POP** page of the second issue of October 19th raised so many disturbing questions that when we visited The Colony again on October 22nd, Shrapnell not only denied us entry but declined to be interviewed even by phone. We had thus had him where we wanted. We could then quote or misquote him at will.

***

There were two contributions in the VOX POP, one of which was written by Istromo, which I knew was bound to irritate Shrapnell. One which insinuated something sinister by misspelling Shrapnell's name said:

It was intriguing to learn that Pastor **Sextus** *Shrapnell had proved happiness not only to the barren and widowed, but even for women whose marriages had broken down because of total neglect which amounted to sexual starvation on the part of their husbands...While we congratulate Pastor for this rare achievement, we are very anxious to know how the sexual desires of these women are satisfied within the confines of the Colony.*

A second article said:

I am interested in knowing who the architect or draughtsman was who designed the buildings of the Colony such that Pastor's house opened to the back to the back door into the widows' and divorcees' chambers, such that anybody could under the cover of darkness move from the women's chamber into the Pastor's and back through the let-in let-out doors, without being detected.

The very next issue of THE NAKED TRUTH continued to focus attention on THE COLONY. The first article on the front page was a brief disclaimer by the publishers. It read:

The name of the pastor at Salvation Colony is not SEXTUS SHRAPNELL, or SEXTOOL SHARPNAIL, but SIXTUS SHRAPNELL. Anybody who for some sinister reason misspells the names to cast aspersions on this undeniably "Holy Man" is doing so at his own risk, and should be ready to shoulder the responsibility which his or her error provokes.

In an inside **VOX POP** article conceived by Ngiawa in the **Job's comforters**' tradition, the reader, purporting to defend Shrapnell said:

I am amazed that we should be so blind. The interview with Pastor Shrapnell indicated that he was taking care, and that he had brought happiness to the deaf, the blind, the lame, the ex-convicts. It did not say he was there to take care only of the interests of women. The emphasis on the pastor's sexual propensities is uncalled for, and unfair. From the good he has done to the inmates of The Colony, it is clear that women, whether divorced or widowed or blind, once they had taken up residence in the Colony were animals in Shrapnell's zoo. They are his just for the beckoning. He did not therefore have to go into that complicated architectural gymnastics just to get them."

Every single thing that was said about The Colony, whether in conscious condemnation or in defence, helped us in that it hurt Pastor Shrapnell as well as his followers and the image of the place. Referring to the much-vaunted Soul to Soul programme, one commentator remarked that:

"Nobody will take such absorbed interest in criminal confession if he himself is not of a criminal disposition. Listening to criminals provides him with a release for his own inherent criminal thoughts!"

Chapter Twenty-Five

Cosmas Mfetebeunu

In a bid to recruit as many detractors of The Colony as we could I went to Dr. Essemo with an autographed copy of the maiden issue of our paper. I had already written to inform him that Shrapnell had ensnared Gertrude, released Bakru from jail and had taken him into the Colony and that the paramours were once more having a good time there. Dr. Essemo was no longer married to Gertrude, but I knew he would feel severely hurt by the fact that his driver should make such a fool of him, and that a blasphemer like Shrapnell would encourage that.

When I went there Dr. Essemo asked me to use the case of Gertrude in a future publication, as an example of the evils being perpetrated by ALCA. The third and subsequent issues of THE NAKED TRUTH carried nothing else but information or more appropriately, misinformation about ALCA and the Colony.

Like all other sects, it was impossible to get a convert out of it. In fact, you ran the risk of ending up as a convert if you were not one of strong convictions about religion. Parents were hurt by their daughters who had virtually carried the religion on their heads. Shrapnell, personally did not prescribe a particular dress for his followers. He constantly castigated flashy outfits and high-heeled shoes because, as he said, they drew undue attention to oneself.

But his Brethren's Keepers who became more strict than himself recommended extremely low hair, the kind the public described as "Crobo"; as for shoes they prescribed sandals; they prescribed white head scarves and down-reaching gowns for women. Cosmetics were banned.

Parents who were anxious to see their daughters look beautiful and well-dressed were scandalized and outraged to see them dressed so absurdly. And the more they tried to dissuade them the more seriously their daughters took to the ALCA prescription.

Other churches, especially the Catholics and Presbyterians who constantly derided ALCA for having no clear-cut scriptural message, stepped in. It was little wonder that Shrapnell had his hands full.

***

I was glad that through our efforts antagonism towards ALCA was gaining ground, and that sooner or later I would be able to convince Mr. Dennis to quit and rejoin his family. So far, even though I knew that behind every sect there was a hidden scandal, I had not yet unearthed enough to discourage Mr. Dennis. It was not enough that parents and husbands detested ALCA. We needed to talk the followers out of it. And that was not easy.

We visited the American Embassy and succeeded in obtaining partial information on Shrapnell. We got addresses of some students studying in the U.S, to whom we sent letters. When the investigation was becoming expensive, we approached Dr. Essemo. That proved to be the turning point because Dr. Essemo had telephone and fax facilities as well as enormous contacts abroad. When he told his friends in the U.S. that the man had wrecked his family the latter went all out to excavate as much damaging information as possible. It was through him that we got the most vital facts. As it turned out, we did not need to superimpose any scandal on Shrapnell because he was all scandal, just the type we were looking for.

We put everything together and the front page of the 25th November issue of our paper was captioned:

WHO EXACTLY IS
REVEREND PASTOR SIXTUS SHRAPNELL?
(See Inside)

Now that we knew who the man was, that inside article was designed to reveal with incontrovertible evidence that Shrapnell was anything but what he professed to be, a true man of God. It said:

The real name of Reverend Pastor Sixtus Shrapnell was Joe Shinburn, once called Dr. Shinburn. Born in 1918 at Congress Valley in the neighbourhood of the University of Witchita in Kansas State in West-Central United States of America. He was the son of retired Reverend Pastor and famous orator and charismatic preacher, Goldsmith Shinburn of the **Church of the Angels of Limbo**, a religious sect that had been founded in America in the early twenties. Joe, as he was usually called, entered the Witchita Medical Academy in 1941, at the age of 23. He graduated as Dental Surgeon in 1948, having taken along with his dental courses, intensive studies in psychiatry and tropical medicine.

In 1953 he moved to Topeka, the capital city of the state.

There, together with three other young doctors they set up a private clinic in Easterling Grove where he was dental surgeon. For five years all went very well for them, and his reputation rose like a meteor.

Then suddenly everything went wrong. In October 1958 he was accused of tempering with the virtues of two of his female patients under the state of anaesthesia. He admitted his guilt, his license was withdrawn and he was banned by the American Medical Association from practising medicine anywhere in America.

He was officially unemployed for four years, during which he spent many months at The Kansas City Hypnotic Centre. In 1963 he was indicted for counterfeiting. In 1965, assuming the name of Sixtus Shrapnell he took to preaching and spent one year in Puerto Rico. In 1967 he went to Cameroon to buy Cameroonian art works.

Nor was that all! At the American Embassy I had tried but failed to get the address of ACCA, Shrapnell's American Council of Churches for Africa. My original intention was to apply to the organization for some form of financial assistance for our publishing ventures. Attempts by phone to friends in the U.S. yielded no fruits. In the end it was established that there was no such organization. This raised one very serious question: where did Shrapnell get the money from that enabled him to realise such goals? Could he have been practising his old trade of counterfeiting again? That was food for thought.

We planted a spy in The Colony.

***

With these new revelations, and as I constantly prayed it should be, Shrapnell and ALCA became the talk of the country in every major newspaper, the target of much adverse criticism.

But our efforts seemed wasted because neither Mr Dennis nor the other followers believed a word of what the papers said. They all, without exception, regarded THE NAKED TRUTH as well as the flood of articles as complete anti-ALCA propaganda machine, disseminating information deliberately designed to influence opinions and actions of individuals or groups with the predetermined end of running down Shrapnell's reputation.

Chapter Twenty-Six

Rev. Father Archibald Danfeely

The fate of the disreputable ALCA pleased us of the Roman Catholic church who featured so prominently in condemning the charlatan Shrapnell. Little did we know that we would soon be facing a scandal of even greater magnitude than that of Shrapnell and his clique. On October 18th, 1972 the private medical consultant to the Menako Diocese established beyond reasonable doubt that Reverend Sister Angela O'Reilly of the Mitsiko parish in the vicinity of Menako was two and a half months pregnant.

On November 1st we, the ten white priests of the three main Menako parishes met in a secret conclave. We were Fathers Ahriman Gracias, Yomael Flush, Theodorus Fredericco, Papiyam Philip, Constantine Mohawk, Michelet Francois, Lavey Newcastle, Gresil Fabrizzio, Ezra Benito and myself, Archibald DanFeely.

The meeting was chaired by our most elderly priest, Father Gresil Fabrizzio, with Lavey Newcastle as the minutes' secretary. Father Mohawk opened the meeting with a long prayer in which he entreated God to send down light so that they would see clearly the way before them, so that the deliberations they were about to engage in should be for the good of all Christendom. He then handed over the floor to the chairman who then began in a manner which indicated that the purpose of the meeting had been already discussed amongst them. He said:

"Fellow brothers in Christ, you will notice that we have decided to keep this secret meeting clean - there's no black priest amongst us this minute.

"We are all God's messengers in this country, but we are no fools. We are not only human, but humans from the quintessential species of humanity. We are white men." He paused and served himself a glass of mineral water.

"It was no accident that Christ was originally white. What I am saying here is that if it lies within our powers to perpetuate the purity of our race and religion, we must put all hands on deck.

"It is now established that Sister Angella O'Reilly of Mitsiko parish whom we all know to be of exemplary conduct in her calling, is two and a half months pregnant - thanks to the hand of the almighty. Let us not make a mistake, for Christendom of the white race shall not forgive us our trespasses if we act unwisely.

"We shall all agree here and now to write a letter to our own white brother, Archbishop Frangle of Ovenga to inform him that we are of the considered opinion that we should stop at nothing to make sure that she is immediately evacuated so that she delivers this Christ in a white land, her own town, Dublin in Ireland."

I sat frozen. He was talking and looking at me as though he had read my thoughts and known that I would oppose him. The way the case was presented, only an enemy of our white race could refuse. They were all unanimous and argued as if they had discussed the matter several times before and were just coming to ratify their discussion.

But the whole idea so pained me that I decided to voice my misgivings. When I raised my finger Father Gresil Fabrizzio seemed not to see it. I kept my hand in the air until he called on me.

"Why don't we try to be realistic for once?" I inquired. "We have spent the best years of our lives on African soil looking for and talking about Christ. Now, on the strength of a mere rumour we are about to take an action which will throw overboard everything we have preached and stood for. What if you carry that your Sister to Ireland or to Jerusalem and she delivers a black child, a black Jesus?"

Father Fabrizzio ordered me to shut up and not bring misfortune on the white world.

"You seem to think it is impossible," I said. "You will be shocked.

"We think that you will instead be shocked," Father Fabrizzio said.

At the end of the meeting a resolution was drawn up and two persons chosen to draft the letter to the Archbishop.

I declined to sign the resolutions.

"Give the African his chance," I said, and then as they walked out I cursed in my throat: "A bishop screws his girlfriend and then people assemble the church to celebrate his achievement!" I know that some of them overheard me, but that did not bother me.

***

Reverend Sister Angela O'reilly

On November 3rd, at 6 pm, Archbishop Felini Frangle paid us of the Menako Diocese a surprise visit on Saturday. He said a scantily attended mass the following day at the Menako Cathedral and at 4 pm he invited me for a private interview at the Father's Rest House.

"I am in receipt, of this letter, dear daughter of Christ," he went straight to the point and read it in detail:

Your Grace;

Even as it was written in the scriptures, that **The Son of Man Shalt Come at a Time When We Are Not Expecting Him...** we the eleven priests of this diocese feel elated to draw the attention of Your Grace, to a startling revelation here surrounding Reverend Sister Angela O'Reilly. We presume that beyond all possible doubts, and call on Your Grace to verify for himself, that Sister Angela O'Reilly, whose dedication to the faith is flawless, has had a rare visitation which may very well be a fulfilment of the Scriptures as foretold in the Holy Book. Unimpeachable Medical authorities have established that Reverend Sister Angela O'Reilly, who has never known a man, is very pregnant.

We are all of one voice, Your Grace, that immediate steps be taken to evacuate Reverend Sister Angela O'Reilly back to Ireland, so that christendom can witness the second coming of Our Lord in a pure environment.

I was wearing my snow-white gown, a white head-tie and a large cross on my neck. I was sitting opposite his Lordship, my right hand over my chest with my right hand holding my left elbow. I was biting my left thumb. When his Lordship had finished talking, I brought my hands together, clasped them and then stretched them between my legs in a tired fashion, the way pregnant women do.

"Sister O'Reilly," the Archbishop resumed, "I have come here to see for myself, and to know for myself because the history of western Christianity takes on a new dimension from this event. But, Sister O'Reilly, permit me to ask you from my heart, are you sure that at no time in your life, within the last six months you have not submitted yourself to desires of the flesh which might in some way result in what we are now considering Divine Visitation? You know what I mean?"

"Your Grace," I began, "how can you conceive of such an idea about me?"

"We are all human," Archbishop Frangle said. "Sisters, brothers, priests, bishops, archbishops, cardinals popes... These are all cloaks that conceal our essential humanity. We are all human. Man is born weak, and in that weakness can fall prey to frailties of all sorts. If you know what I mean."

I stretched again tiredly, closed my eyes, then opened them and stared at the Archbishop inquiringly. My head drooped and with tears clouding my eyes I responded:

"Your Grace, may I, in all honesty, admit that I am pregnant. I do not know how the Blessed Virgin Mary felt, but I am pregnant without having known any man. Whatever has happened to me, Your Grace, has the hand of God in it. If the Lord has chosen me as the vehicle through which to manifest his divinity, I cannot choose but accept," I ended up with a feeling of achievement.

Archbishop Frangle Felinni looked at me for a long time, smacked his lips and asked:

"Is Sister O'Reilly insisting that I should believe, and consequently the entire Christendom should believe, that it is true that through you the Lord will effect his second coming?"

I nodded in silence.

"Revelation 22,12" he recited to himself.

"Listen! I am coming soon. I will bring my rewards with me, to give to each one according to what he has done. I am the first and the last, the beginning and the end."

"We just have to believe, Your Grace."

"If what you are causing us to believe turns out to be false, Sister O'Reilly, then you shall have brought shame and dishonour to the white race in particular and to the entire Catholic church in particular."

Chapter Twenty-Seven

Commissioner Chemogh Fuofinkwo

On November 15th, Commissioner Chemogh Fuofinkwo of the Ovenga Emi-Immigration received an anonymous letter:

Dear Mr. Commissioner;

This information is confidential but all important because it is coming from the inner circle of the church. I choose to remain anonymous because I do not want to suffer the fate of Father Danfeely. Get this straight: Reverend Sister Angela O'Reilly of the Mitsiko parish is three months pregnant. It has been established that it is the will of God, and that it may very well end up in the Second Coming of Christ. The white priests are making plans to evacuate her on any pretexts of health, so that she delivers Christ not in Africa where they have spent years looking for him, but in Ireland where they think he ought to be born.

If you think the way the writer of this letter does, that our people have also suffered enough to deserve the birth of Christ on their soil, use your good office to ensure that that lady does not leave this country before nine months are over.

On November 10th, it had been reported that Reverend Father Archibald Danfeely of the Menako main parish had been found dead, most probably of a heart attack, in his bathroom. The Archbishop was said to have ordered that arrangements be made for his burial the very next day, and that no autopsy be performed on the body.

The Archbishop himself was said to have been present at the burial, as if to ensure that the corpse had actually been buried. In his funeral speech he is said to have described Father Danfeely as: "a noble pillar of his calling, a man whose death had created a gap in the diocese which will not be easy to fill because he gave his body and soul to the service of the church."

The anonymous letter coupled with circumstances of the death of the priest caused me to summon a meeting of my top collaborators. The sudden death and hasty burial without post mortem examination of Father Danfeely was reviewed and a small committee set up to look into the matter and make suggestions. At the end of the day I dispatched a message to the Menako sector.

On the 16th of November I sent this brief invitation to Reverend Sister Angela O'Reilly:

Dear Sister O'Reilly;

You are urgently invited to this office for a matter concerning you. Kindly bring along your identification documents, passport and the like.

I knew Sister Angella O'Reilly would think that the invitation was part of the plot to secret her out of the country. She came without consulting the views of any of the white priests. When she came and handed over her passport and church identity card, I knew I had got her. That Jesus would have to be delivered on our own soil, I told myself. I examined them for a long time and then put them in a drawer. I then told her in a freezing tone:

"We will get back to you sooner or later."

I was informed that the priests of the nearby parishes learned of the event with consternation and alarm. But that did not bother me. When Father Fabrizzio called at my Police Station I told him that we were looking into the matter, and that the officer handling the investigations had gone on leave.

The Archbishop at Ovenga was immediately contacted. When he went up to our service and complained that the passport of an ailing Reverend Sister had been confiscated, the Commissioner who had been sufficiently briefed on the scandal told him:

"Your Grace, this is a very delicate matter and we want to handle it with extreme care. We have never had any problem whether with the church or with your person. The press is heavily on our backs to say something about it. We have been reluctant to do so.

"If you do not leave it in our hands, we shall hand over the matter to them to use it in whatever way they wish."

***

The threat was unnecessary because I noticed that the editors of THE NAKED TRUTH had been served a copy of the letter that had been sent to me. On receiving the tell-tale letter the editor had made just a few inquiries and had concluded that it was no rumour. The front page caption of the November 20th issue of the paper was:

MURDER IN HIGH PLACES:

FATHER ARCHIBALD DANFEELY'S HEART-ATTACKED WHILE CATHOLICS PREPARE TO EVACUATE REVEREND SISTER TO DELIVER CHRIST IN IRELAND.

SECURITY NOOSE TIGHTENS AROUND MOTHER OF CHRIST (See Inside)

The inside story was as spicy and interesting as the young journalists could possibly make it. It told of the death from their own standpoint, filling in gaps wherever they thought necessary. Although they too did not establish whether the pregnancy had a serious religious dimension to it, they made a telling point. They warned that it was important for Sister

O'Reilly to be protected because a Catholic clique may not sit back, fold its arms and see Christ delivered in Africa. They would rather lose that Christ and His mother!

Whether this was mere speculation to sell their paper or well-founded fears, they were proven right. On December 1st, Sister O'Reilly, with all the security that we had set up surrounding her, was found dead in her bedroom.

Chapter Twenty-Eight

Istromo Ngiawa: Master Planner

Cosmas and myself worked indefatigably to link the Catholic Church scandal with that of ALCA. Our purpose, as before was to prove to Dennis that religion of any sort was not a thing in which to invest one's emotional capital, or a venture for which one would sacrifice one's family life.

Sheer luck continued to convert us into miracle workers. While we were digging out more information on the O'Reilly saga, fresh material was received from our contacts in the U.S. which transformed Shrapnell into a wanted man, an outright criminal.

Another fax sent to Dr. Essemo revealed that during the four years that Shrapnell was not officially employed he had set up a counterfeiting business. He printed bills which were said to be even better than the genuine ones. He had then set up a fake brokerage in the heart of Topeka, through which he put the money into circulation. That was how he came by so much money to travel with and then begin his God's work in Africa.

We stored up every vital and incriminating information, doling it out in bits in each new issue of THE NAKED TRUTH. We concluded that even if he had made very much money, he could not have made enough to enable him realise his gigantic project. We therefore set out to investigate the local source of his wealth.

It was just as scandalous. He was definitely secretly continuing with his counterfeiting business. He had two accounts at the People's Bank. He personally deposited huge sums of new notes once in a while. But generally when he wanted money he sent somebody with a cheque or cheques.

***

While we were tightening the noose and constricting Shrapnell more and more, we kept an ear on developments in the O'Reilly case. It was established soon after O'Reilly's death that she had not been killed by a Catholic clique as originally intimated. She had killed herself because of shame. A strict investigation into her movements indicated an incident which had hitherto been taken for granted.

On October 10th she had reported at ALL FOR LOVE CLINIC for an emergency: she had violent tooth ache. Why she had chosen the clinic was never to be known. But, that was the same clinic in which Shrapnell rendered free services in dental care and surgery.

It was also established that on the day she visited the clinic, Shrapnell whom she had never seen before and whom she may never have heard of before, attended to her. Dr. Chopawuf had a consultation elsewhere in town. The nurses on duty recall that Shrapnell had spent a long time with her, that he had certainly administered anaesthesia. But they swore that they did not know if Shrapnell (who was used to such tricks!) did anything extraordinary to her while in the state of anaesthesia. At the time these details were dug up, Sister O'Reilly was three months pregnant. Three months back from that date put the pregnancy at just around the day she visited ALL FOR LOVE CLINIC.

It was this recent disclosure which drove Sister Angela O'Reilly to kill herself with an overdose of nivaquine.

***

Findings from the O'Reilly case which the Catholic Church fought a losing battle to kill, definitely helped in the annihilation of Shrapnell.

As is usual with people in authority who have something to hide, Shrapnell began by calling the findings "tissues of absurdities, a senseless pack of lies" that will lead nobody anywhere. He and his die-hard followers denied every single charge, dismissing them as "lies fabricated to tarnish the image of a man who had done what the government itself could not do."

In the December 13th issue of THE NAKED TRUTH we suggested that Shrapnell summon a press conference to clear himself. We did very well in blowing up the scandals. We were glad to find that Shrapnell's followers, especially the twelve Keepers who had all stood behind him in discounting all the allegations began to get so worried by the accusations that they too urged him to call a press conference to save the face of ALCA from further embarrassment.

In the December 22nd issue we on our own declared that Shrapnell had finally agreed to call a conference on the 24th of December, to which the public was invited to know the truth.

As soon as this issue was in circulation, and as soon as we were sure that copies must have reached the Colony, Cosmas and myself paid the last visit to the Colony, the visit which we were sure would send Dennis packing out of the damned place back to his wife and children.

By this time Shrapnell had become incommunicado. He had given instructions forbidding anybody to enter or leave the Colony without his expressed permission.

Chapter Twenty-Nine

Cosmas Mfetebeunu

I telephoned from the vicinity of **The Colony**. I had no other reason than that I wanted to talk to Mr. Dennis.

We received no answer. As we were to learn later, Shrapnell had ordered the line to be cut off. I therefore decided that we write a brief note to Mr. Dennis informing him that we had come to tell him something of extreme importance. In our mind we knew that we were bringing the kind of news that would bring peace to **The Colony** and save everybody from embarrassment. And, above all, such information was bound to finally convince Mr. Dennis to leave the place and rejoin his wife and children.

In the morning of that day, having put all the pieces of our investigations together I was so excited that I could not help telephoning my sister. I had reassured her that we had in our hands information, the disclosure of which would send Mr. Dennis packing out of **The Colony**.

What shocked me was the fact that my sister received the news with very little excitement. She sounded in my ears as though she did not want to meet her husband. It looked like I was the one who stood to gain by having him out of there, and not herself. I seemed to be weeping more than the bereaved.

When the note was delivered to Mr. Dennis he left to meet us. without informing anybody. From the small window in his apartment through which Shrapnell usually spied on those who came in and went out, he saw Mr. Dennis leave.

But, even though he had become extremely paranoid and very distrustful of everybody, he had nothing against Mr. Dennis to the extent of stopping him from leaving The Colony. Besides, had he wanted to, it would have been hard because the mounting pressure on him to resign had robbed him of all his strength of purpose. The conflicting emotions, to conceal his guilt without looking aggressive or behaving so, virtually paralysed him. Some force, that will power that had caused him to inspire people to move mountains, had suddenly gone out of him.

***

"We would like to advise you to withdraw from this organization, this night," I began.

"Why this night?"

"You have read the papers about this your God..."

"I read some. Others I did not read," Mr. Dennis said, "mainly because we have all concluded that you are just fabricating lies to tarnish the image of Our Father."

Mr. Dennis took his time before talking.

"Moyo, Mr. Dennis," I called, "are you aware that Reverend Shrapnell assisted occasionally in the ALL FOR LOVE CLINIC in town?"

"Once in a while, yes. I know that Dr. Valdas Chopawuf is his friend of old, from what he told me personally," he added.

"What you may not know is that he was the one who attended to Sister O'Reilly, that Roman Catholic Reverend Sister whose pregnancy has brought so much embarrassment to the entire Christian Church in Africa."

Mr. Dennis tilted his head in disbelief and stared at me with a mixture of dismay and fresh concern.

"You mean who attended to the sister? We are talking of two persons here."

"I mean Pastor Shrapnell."

"What can this mean?" he asked.

"Perhaps this other bit will throw more light on that. Reverend Shrapnell once ran a dental clinic in Kansas state in the U.S. He was accused of having sex with two patients he had put in a state of anaesthesia."

Mr. Dennis raised his eye brows in a surprise that almost amounted to horror, and then nodded grimly, smacked his lips and shook his head. There was only one person who knew that Pastor Shrapnell had once been a surgeon. That one person was Dr. Valdas Chopawuf. And even Dr. Chopawuf did not know precisely why Shrapnell no longer practised. All he knew was that Shrapnell "had decided to cure the souls and not the flesh," as he himself often said. Pastor Shrapnell had once shown him a copy of his professional certificate and, on the strength of that Chopawuf who was himself a dental nurse who passed for a dental doctor, had sought Shrapnell's advice on several occasions in complicated cases of surgery.

There were times when Shrapnell was actually permitted to carry out consultations and make prescriptions. This usually happened when whites booked to see Dr. Chopawuf, and he feared to put his reputation on the line.

Reverend Sister Angella O'Reilly had booked to see Dr. Chopawuf because he was a white dentist, and Dr. Chopawuf had hired the expertise of Shrapnell because he wanted to impress a patient who was coming there for the first time.

Shrapnell's proficiency in medicine, however, remained a secret unknown even to his closest associates in **The Colony**. All they knew was that he visited hospitals and clinics to preach the word of God to the afflicted, the sick and the dying. In fact, it was this secret that strengthened the faith in him of many of his die-hard adherents. He would boast that with faith in God a preacher was as good as an even better than a doctor. Sister Rebecca who was the first woman to be appointed into the enviable rank of Brethren's Keeper, was a case in point.

***

It was common practice for church men to visit the sick in hospital and talk to them on Sundays. Once, when Shrapnell was visiting the Menako General Hospital and talking to patients he found the woman in deep pain. The doctors were baffled by her case which they had tried very unsuccessfully to diagnose. The woman had been twice taken from the hospital to a traditional doctor. Finding that she could not be cured she had been brought back to the hospital. She was the wife of the Secretary General to the Provincial Governor, and she was at the point of being evacuated to London when Shrapnell showed up.

At the height of his glory in Kansas Shrapnell had once been described by the *Journal of American Medical Association* as a "diagnostic wizard," and in another article he was called "a bedside sleuth," both of which compliments drew attention to the fact that he had a way of diagnosing an illness that baffled ordinary medical practitioners.

Having watched her intently for a while and having talked to her about Jesus, Shrapnell pulled out one of his diagnostic tricks. Grasping the woman's toe for an instant he waved good-bye, and as soon as they were out of earshot he told his startled followers and the two doctors who had been admiring him:

"The Lord tells me what she has. Lead her to **The Colony**."

There was hesitation for a whole day until the woman herself became very anxious to go there. She sent for her husband and insisted that they take her there just for a prayer session. That was done. When she arrived he took his bible in his left hand, placed his right hand on her shoulder and prayed for a minute. Then he wrote down on a piece of paper:

"This woman has a leakage of a heart valve."

He was proven right when her case was re-diagnosed at the University Teaching Hospital. When she survived, she became an ardent follower of Shrapnell, while the hospital doctors stood in awe. But the diagnosis of Madam Rebecca was scientific, not mysterious as he made everybody belief.

From his training in the medical school and later during private practice, he was aware that patients suffering from leakage of a heart valve or this particular heart condition cause a distinctive jerky pulse, easily observed in the big toe. Thus did his reputation grow as a divine healer.

Chapter Thirty

Cosmas Mfetebeunu

The state of medical practice in the country helped make him a divine healer. The medical school graduated at least 50 general practitioners every year. Except for a handful who proceeded for specialization courses thereafter in Britain, America, Kenya and Nigeria, the lot of them who occupied the offices of chief medical officers, delegates of health, or opened clinics, built mansions and rode expensive cars, were no better than staff nurses by British and American medical standards where the health of citizens is taken seriously. Though admission was supposed to be based on academic performance at the entrance examination, the entire examination exercise was widely known to be a mere formality. The list of candidates sent in by highly placed government officials and businessmen was usually so long that it was usually unnecessary to consult the list made up of those who had actually passed the exam. Attention was focused mainly on so-called "pressure cases."

The result was that such "native doctors" (as they were disparagingly called) generally gambled over the most eliminatory cases. And so, with prayer in the forefront, Sixtus passed for a miracle worker. He would visit a patient with a bad case and quickly diagnose the sickness, during his evangelising visits to the hospital. He would then send somebody to cause the patient to be brought before him. When that was done, knowing full well what the problem was, and knowing full well how the patient would be treated, he would cause those present to sing the miracle-working song:

"Prayer is the Key, prayer is the key, prayer is the master key. *Jesus started with prayers and ended with   prayers, prayer is the master key.*"

Invariably, the patient became a convert after treatment. Thus did it turn out that many of his ardent supporters were people who owed their lives to him, and his God, of course.

These were secrets that but for our painstaking investigations, would never have been known by anybody but Shrapnell himself, alone. Mr. Dennis had never regretted working with Shrapnell. He had embraced his teaching and ideas with his whole heart. He had come to him friendless, wifeless, homeless. And Shrapnell had given even more than he had expected to find.

His present happiness and calmness of mind was no figment of the imagination. It was a stark reality which everybody could see. All the brethren were of the same disposition. They took him for what they knew, a man of God. When, therefore we mentioned the case of the reverend sister, Mr. Denis found it hard to believe.

"Are you saying that is what might have happened to that Sister?" he inquired.

"That is what happened. There is ample proof."

Mr. Dennis squeezed his lower lip and blinked copiously, nervously.

"It was when his license was withdrawn that he became a preacher."

Mr. Dennis smiled a bit.

"Listen to this too. There is no such organization as **American Council of Churches for Africa** which was said to be the major sponsor of ALCA in general and the Salvation Colony in particular."

"How then does he have the money to do all this?"

"Which brings me to the next point. Reverend Shrapnell is a counterfeiter of the first water. He has in this colony a counterfeiting machine. Do you know that there is a part of Shrapnell's apartment called "The Holy of Holies?"

Mr. Dennis smiled but said nothing.

"In the People's Bank at Menako," I went on, "he has struck a deal with the cashier of Counter Three, one Christophersin Ezubura. Under those terms, Ezubura accepts the false currency and deposits genuine money into account **No. MN/001112234. F**rom this account he withdraws his millions in the name of the nonexistent ACCA."

Mr. Dennis' blood seemed to freeze as if he had been dipped into ice-cold water. It was as though he was dreaming, and for a while he thought I had taken leave of my senses. Was ALCA an organization to promote heinous crimes? he must have wondered. Like a hen bathing in saw dust he shook his head briskly and closed and opened his eyes to find it a dream. No, it was a stark reality. Still bent on disbelieving the allegation, Mr. Dennis rubbed his hands over his head, pressed his lower lip again with his left thumb and forefinger for a long time.

"What if the answers to all those questions is 'No'?" he asked.

"It cannot be NO," I said with defiant certainty. "It cannot be NO. What if the answers are YES?" I asked Mr. Dennis.

"Reverend Shrapnell is an Angel. That is why we call him Our Father. He is a man of God. Our saviour."

"And so?" I inquired.

"But the man you are describing to me is a monster, a devil, not the man who has brought so much joy to our hearts, not Our Father!"

"That is nothing but the truth, the whole truth. What if we tell you that one of those your so-called 'Brethren' was an informant, and that he has told us all about what was going on behind your back?"

Mr. Dennis smiled tiredly.

"When you first went in to talk to Pastor Shrapnell, did somebody not receive you at the porch?"

"And so?"

"Did that man not talk to you first?"

"And so?"

"That man carried a small pocket tape recorder with him in which he secretly recorded all your conversation with him."

Mr. Dennis looked across at me and smiled again.

"Before you went in he had already given the cassette to Shrapnell, who had already played it to himself. He had therefore known your areas of interest and could afford to talk about it in a manner which made him look like a God."

Mr. Dennis said nothing.

"That man is no God. He is just a smart guy, that's all. This man knows that there are things you would discuss with his servant which you dare not discuss with him. So he has to look for a means of getting access to this information and then use it the way he wants."

Mr. Dennis breathed in and out. He would give Shrapnell the benefit of the doubt, it seemed. Until...

"We are waiting. Go to him with any of your men and talk to him. If he refutes only one of these several charges I shall call the press conference myself to confess that all the allegations are false. But, moyo Dennis, remember that you have only until this night to pull out honourably or be shamed and damned together."

Chapter Thirty-One

Dennis Nunqam Ndendemajem

I returned to **The Colony** in a smouldering irritation, my temperature, pulse and tongue, all speaking of a dreadful crisis. This was going to be the most difficult decision to make, and so I tried to impart form on my tormenting thoughts. How was I, a mere mortal, going to confront the Man of God, the defender of the weak, my own personal saviour, the man in the absence of whom I would have long perished in a gutter for want of a place to stay and food to eat?

Yet, it was necessary. Whatever I was going to say (and that weighed on me like a bag of cement!) was for the good of **The Colony**, not because I believed the rumours. Reverend Pastor Sixtus Shrapnell must take it in the light in which I myself viewed it - as the only means of dispelling all the unfounded accusations made against ALCA.

With the important exception of our Father himself, we the members of the colony scarcely travelled out of its confines, unless on a crusade. We usually had no reason to travel out. We had everything inside. It therefore did not take me a long time to summon the eleven others to whom I revealed what I had just learnt.

My brethren were unanimous in decrying the allegations as false information calculated to tarnish the good name of an organization which has achieved for the citizens of this country what the government could never achieve. I drew their attention to the newspaper reports with which they were all very familiar. I then formulated some five or so questions, the answers to which might make us rethink our attitude towards Our Father.

"It cannot be," they all shouted when I listed the questions to them. Unbending devotion to Our Father had long robbed us of the powers to think for ourselves. Whatever he condemned was what we condemned. We praised only what he praised. Since he had passed his judgment on the newspaper articles and the rumours as wickedly false accusations, this judgment had long become ours too.

Many of us, in fact all of us, were so convinced of Our Father's innocence that we thought it would be the height of folly, blatant blasphemy, for us to even approach Our Father with the problem. We asked ourselves several times: "if it turns out that He is in fact not as guilty as the public and the press was saying, will he not call on God to burn us alive as He had once threatened?"

The counterfeiting part of the accusation bothered me very much. If He was a counterfeiter as it was claimed from the Cosmas' report, why would the government not arrest him right away? We could not understand. The whole world was behind Our Father, or at least used to be behind Him, we all recalled, until the press turned against Him.

Because we were not all agreed on what to do, somebody suggested that we put the matter to vote. We agreed and did so by a show of hands. Six brethren voted in favour of going to confront Our Father. Six voted against. There was a second round of voting. This time, I who had voted against the showdown changed sides and voted in favour. With this narrow margin, the twelve of us took what we knew deep in our hearts of hearts to be the greatest risk of our lives to challenge Our **God**. I was nominated the spokesman on the issue. I accepted. I did not like accusations one bit, and so was very anxious to have the matter resolved once and for all.

***

The continuous appearance of articles in the papers as well as the spreading of rumours by word of mouth against our church turned Our Father into something different. I had even begun to sense that he was looking at some of us with intense suspicion. One day, from the way he suddenly started behaving towards me, I asked myself whether he thought I shared Cosmas' feelings towards our church, since he was my brother-in-law.

The stories about the place hurt us all, but it seemed to eat Our Father up like a canker worm. I could not believe my eyes. He, who had always taught us to fear no one but God, seemed now to fear everybody. He complained that the whole world was after him. He became increasingly unpredictable, moody and even insolent. This bothered us very much.

He preferred to be left more and more alone and behaved as if it was he who needed help and no longer us His flock. On our part, I and my brethren had been too preoccupied with defending His person and the reputation of ALCA to know how the accusations weighed on Him.

***

When I entered His room Our Father received me with unusual coldness. This sent my fears rising high into the sky. Intuitively Our Father knew that the journalists had spoken to me, and immediately suspected that some hidden truth might have been made known to me by them.

"What is the problem?" he asked. I noticed a sudden rush of resentment and aggression in his voice.

"No problem as such, Our Father," I said. I was particularly careful to be polite. "Only that our Brethren's Keepers will like to talk to you on something important for the life of this Colony."

I saw Our Father's brows come together. He half-rose and then fell back. His eyes grew dimmer and downcast and his nose instantly turned red. In a hoarse voice and with painful dejection written all over his face he asked:

"When do they want to see me? Is it about the press-conference?"

"It concerns the conference too, Our Father," I told Him. "They can see you now," I added. "The sooner the better."

"No, they will not see me," He said. His voice was charged with anxiety and irritation and even hate. I took mental note that it was the first time Our Father had openly exhibited such conduct, the very first time He had objected to a suggestion that I had ever made. I was looking directly into His eyes. I felt a certain blankness in my own face as though I could no longer comprehend the reality engulfing me.

It was as if Our Father was reading my thoughts because He immediately reconsidered the answer. "Let me see them at 5 pm," he said. "I need some rest," he said as an afterthought.

"No problem, Our father," I said politely and walked out.

"Brother Dennis," He called after me. When I came back He inquired: "Do you have any idea of what the whole thing is about?"

For the first time I found it difficult to conceal my irritation. "That is an answer that the whole group has to give you together," I said.

He too sensed my vexation. "I hope you have not joined my enemies to make a fool of me" he said, foreboding, by gesturing threateningly, pacing up and down, muttering to Himself and striking his breast with his right fist.

"Your enemies are our enemies, Our Father," I pointed out. "Anybody who tries to hurt or slander you, slanders us. We take it personal." I then walked me out and away. But Our Father's attitude worried me like a pebble in my shoe.

He had always taught us never to lose our heads, never to lose our patience or our calm. And we had always accepted this. It had become our way of living. Now He seemed to be violating his very principles.

This thought brought other thoughts to my mind.

It began to filter into my troubled mind that quite a few times I had sensed something intensely mysterious about Our Father. I had personally noticed once or twice that He who generally put on a gay look, could suddenly switch from the height of gaiety and excitement into instant moodiness as though he had suddenly recalled some sad event from the past. He had a temperament that could by turns become cold and violent, reckless and cautious.

Then the counterfeiting issue crossed my mind again, turning it into gall, into mud. If Our Father were accused of a sexual offence, I could understand because sex was a crime of passion, and Our Father, I had long discovered, was passionate in extremes in whatever he did. If He were accused of alcohol I could understand because I found Him sipping some whisky a few times before a crusade.

Not counterfeiting, I told myself. It was too much of a criminal offense to be associated with a man of God. Counterfeiting, I contemplated, was never committed by accident. It was not something a man could claim he did in ignorance. A counterfeiter was somebody who went into it knowing it was a crime. A counterfeiter had to be somebody who devoted much time and money and equipment... No, that was not something to pin onto a man of God. It was inconceivable that Reverend Pastor Sixtus Shrapnell, Our Father, would do any such thing, I concluded. If it was already so well known that Shrapnell was a counterfeiter to the extent that journalists were talking about it, why should the government not arrest him? But again, the gnawing question, why should he suddenly become aggressive towards me? Did He actually have something to hide?

Chapter Thirty-Two

Dennis Nunqam Ndendemajem

O ur Father shall not receive us now," I reported back.

"When shall he receive us?" I was asked.

"At five p.m.," I said resignedly. "He will only receive us at five pm," I added.

"Why?" they asked.

"Why? He is resting," I told them. What else could I say? After all, was that not what he had said?

There was a deep silence across the room.

"Let this not be true, what we are hearing," one of our brethren said.

"God forbid," I said.

There was a slight sign of relief on their faces until another Brethren stepped in.

"But, let us say the impossible happens," echoed the fears of all of us, "and it turns out that the press is right?"

"The press has never been right anywhere," I said, fighting to console myself, praying deep in my heart that whatever disturbing information we were receiving was actually false. My brethren were looking at me and I could imagine the gravity and sombreness which had implanted itself in my visage. I felt somewhat grief-stricken.

We retired to our separate activities. Five o'clock was two hours away, but with minds ridden with quavering anxiety, it looked like two years for, we were all impatient to meet Our Father and clear the air. I strolled out of the camp and down the road where I went up to the young journalists.

"We shall be talking to him about it at five," I said and immediately turned and went back.

In the breeze that was blowing violently through the leaves I could hear a very faint answer from Cosmas: "We shall wait." It was as if he was talking to himself.

***

At four o'clock the radio announced:

"The controversy surrounding the status of Salvation Colony would be cleared tomorrow morning. The controversial Reverend Pastor Sixtus Shrapnell has agreed to hold a press conference in the grounds of worship in **The Colony** *at 10 a.m. The public and pressmen are invited to have their doubts cleared."*

Our Father, no doubt, followed the announcement. During the two hours that he had to wait to receive his twelve disciples he had made up his mind. If the press has brought pressure to bear on the public to harass his innocent followers, he would teach the world a lesson. He was not going back to America in shame. If Salvation Colony was going to end, it must be he himself to end it, whenever he wants. He would unmake what he has made, period.

The bile of seven pythons which had been killed during construction work had been handed over to him for burial because it was said it was deadly poisonous. That was going to be his press conference. He would have one last drink with his disciples and the world will remember his last supper!

***

At five o'clock precisely the twelve of us entered Our Father's chamber. There was the faintest whiff of perfume mixed with alcohol in the air. A syringe lay suspiciously in a tray at the foot of the table near his lounge chair. He may have administered one of those things he usually administered before a major crusade. His eyes and entire body were unusually red, his hair unkempt and his shirt buttoned only to just below the breast, showing his very hairy chest.

He looked like a man at war with himself. A small golden crucifix was lying against a bible on the table before him. He rose, shook our hands briskly and showed us where to sit. He was the one who spoke first.

"I hope that you have not finally joined my enemies to make a fool of me?" he asked, his eyes darting from one face to another. With displeasure I noticed that his fingers were trembling as he spoke! He himself must have sensed it, for he clenched his fist soon after he started speaking.

The question took everyone of us by surprise. When I looked round I could see that a look of complete astonishment and perplexity had implanted itself on every face.

"Why, Our Father?" I inquired in a deeply regretful voice. "You make us worried," I told him frankly. "I said before and I am saying here again that your enemies, if they exist, are our enemies."

"Did you follow the 4 o'clock news?" he asked from a tangent, his countenance flushing darkly and uneasily. We had been praying we should not be the ones to tell him about the announcement

"We did, Our Father," I answered.

He adjusted his owl spectacles and inquired:

"And what do you make of it?"

Deliberately and without the slightest show of worry or nervousness, I said:

"We think it the best thing to do, for the good of this Colony. It will restore some respect, and some hope. The amount of foul talk in the air is disturbing."

Our Father nodded. There was in his eyes the looks of one who had suddenly discovered some treachery against his person. He sat rather still for an uncomfortable moment, his narrow eyes with pupils fixed on me, widened as he surveyed us his once so faithful followers sceptically over his glasses.

"Who of you sent in that announcement to the effect that I had agreed to hold a press conference here tomorrow?" he inquired with pensive persistence.

We all looked round at each other in consternation.

"We thought Our Father did," I said.

"I didn't," He said, anger creeping rapidly into his voice. "I did not. I could not summon an event in which ingrates would come and insult me. I thought one of you did."

We all shook our heads.

"It must be the work of the press again," he said.

"Might be," somebody said.

"At any rate, what have you come for?" he inquired impatiently.

Once again we looked on, stunned.

"Your reaction amazes us immensely," I pointed out. "We are your close collaborators in the running of this colony. We have met hundreds of times in the past to discuss ways and means of improving the place. Why is this particular meeting so different from any other?"

I could not quite understand the cause of his aggression. Why this sudden suspicion? Did Our Father really have something to hide? What could that be? I continued to wonder.

"Ask yourselves" He snapped remorselessly, perspiration mingling with perfume and alcohol in the air. "At any rate what have you come for? I am sorry I may be overreacting."

There was a silence during which Shrapnell rose to his fridge and took out a kettle which he placed on the table. He reached for a dozen plastic cups from his cupboard and poured each of them a drink which might have been orange juice or something of the sort. He did not serve himself. When he sat back I rose and served him the drink too.

As if by previous arrangement, nobody drank. We would discover after his death that the drink contained the bile of one of the several pythons we killed during construction work. But the main reason we did not drink was because we were stunned by our leader's reactions which were beginning to make us think that the press may, after all, not be totally wrong. If only one of the allegations was true, it was very bad news for **The Colony**, each of us thought in his heart.

Shrapnell too did not drink. Adopting a more positive and determined tone I said:

"Our Father, as I said before, we do not know who sent in the radio announcement, but we think that press conference absolutely necessary. We shall be on your side to the end of the world because you have made us see another home in Jesus, having abandoned our wives, children and the like. We would like you to hold that press conference. We shall be on your side. The whole world is on your side except a few jealous beings. But while we prepare to answer any questions with you, we have four questions to ask you. We have had a rather long debate as to whether we should ask you or not. In the end, majority carried the vote."

Shrapnell breathed in and out, every bit of concentration now focused on concealing a sudden feeling of guilt. Knowing what he truly was, and knowing what we thought or took him to be, Shrapnell always took exquisite care to preserve and project that image of piety he had created in our church. Protecting and projecting that image were the cornerstones of everything he did whether in church or in **The Colony**, and he protected this with the zeal and cunning of a fox.

His luck, most unexpectedly, appeared to be running out. He went into his bathroom and returned with a towel with which he mopped his face. He opened the fridge, took out a small coke which he opened and drank from the bottle.

"Cheers," he said and lifted the bottle. The twelve of us lifted our cups and then, with that impending sense of doom sinking deeper and deeper into our hearts, we placed the cups back on the stools by our sides, but without drinking.

"Who were those who voted for, and those who voted against?" Shrapnell asked.

"It does not matter, Our Father," I answered for all of us. "What is important is the question we have brought."

"It is written in Matthew 10, verses 16 to 20," Shrapnell began as I looked away. *Behold I send you out as sheep in the midst of wolves. Therefore be wise as serpents and harmless as doves.*

"But beware of men for they will deliver you up to councils and scourge you in their synagogues.

You will be brought before governors and kings for my sake, as a testimony to the gentiles.' What is your question?" Shrapnell asked looking furiously into our bewildered eyes.

"First question, Our Father, it is being rumoured that you were the dentist on duty on October 10th, the day the Roman Catholic Reverend Sister O'Reilly who is now pregnant visited the ALL FOR LOVE clinic in town. Is that true?"

Shrapnell sneered ludicrously. He was obviously horror-stricken for a split second. His eyes started from their hooded sockets. And then he growled in a trembling voice and with a startled gaze he asked:

"What if I was on duty? Matthew chapter 10 verse 35 tells you: '*I have come to set a man against his father, a daughter against her mother, and a daughter-in-law against her mother-in-law.*"

I, suppressing a shiver paid no heed to the quotation. "Then it will lead us to the second question..." I continued mercilessly.

"Which is?"

I was silent for a long time. The response and the fear that Shrapnell could be guilty scattered my thoughts. I searched my mind for a while and then continued:

"Which is, whether Reverend Pastor Sixtus Shrapnell had a hand in that lady's pregnancy which has brought so much humiliation to the Christian church in Africa."

Shrapnell looked round our group of his most faithful followers and shook his head.

"I have said it before," he began. "Speak the truth and speak it ever. He that hides the wrong he does, does the wrong thing still."

"Our Father, meaning?"

"Good and evil are two sides of the same coin, man," he said, his voice echoing distinctly in the reigning stillness that had assailed the room, "a perfectly good man is capable of the vilest evil, just by turning the other side of the coin." He smiled to himself and then said what we feared he might say: "I am human," he spat out, his eyes squinting with unjustified vexation." I was tempted. I did. What is your second question?"

The dark cords of my emotions drew taut. For a brief moment my countenance underwent a transformation from a softness to a hardness before softening again into one of uncontrollable sadness. Then it tightened again, and I met Shrapnell's eyes with a look of undisguised contempt and disgust.

I sighed and shook my head in unspeaking agitation.

"The second question, Our Father, is whether there is any such thing as **The American Council of Churches for Africa** from which you receive financial support to run this colony."

"There is no such organization," Shrapnell said nonchalantly, arousing the total astonishment of all of us. "What is the third question?"

I felt the back of my scalp contract, my mind suddenly becoming a welter of conflicting emotions and with my tongue trembling insanely I asked:

"Was Pastor Shrapnell once a practising Dentist, and if so why was his licence withdrawn?"

Shrapnell bit his lower lip with a sad smile and said:

"Reverend Pastor Sixtus Shrapnell was never a practising dentist anywhere on this planet. And if he ever was his licence was never withdrawn." It was actually my fault. At the time he was dentist and at the time his licence was withdrawn, the man we were now calling Shrapnell was called Joe Shinburn.

I hesitated and then asked the next question:

"Does Reverend Pastor Sixtus Shrapnell know a certain Christophersin Ezubura, cashier of the third counter in the People's Bank in Menako."

"I know him," he responded, his nimble fingers clenching and unclenching rapidly, nervously, ominously.

"Finally did you ever strike a deal with him by which some false money could be deposited into account no. MN/001112234?"

***

"Like father like son," goes the famous adage. Joe Shinburn learned a lot from his father who was not only a preacher but also an engraver. The daily harassment he watched his father go through every morning and evening at the hands of creditors inculcated in him at a very early age a lifelong fear of insolvency.

Like his father and grandparents, he was a gifted artist. At the age of 8, he was drawing pictures of his parents and sketching street scenes in his Witchita neighbourhood. But he was more than an artist; he was equipped with what amounted to photographic sight. He could look at a face or an object, study it for a minute or so, and then reproduce it on paper without so much as glancing at it a second time. When he was only 10, Joe was so good at briefly studying a signature and then reproducing it that people from all over Witchita asked him to reproduce their signatures and then stood in open-mouthed admiration at the feat.

He discovered by sheer coincidence that his father engraved bills. He was only 12 then. Successfully pretending that he knew nothing of what was happening he acquired the art - a sound knowledge of inks, dyes and bleaches. He could bleach a $5 bill white without destroying the paper.

A meticulous counterfeiting craftsman, he possessed such an acute olfactory sense that he could make bogus money smell exactly like real money. That was how he earned a living during the four years that he was unemployed in Topeka after his dismissal from the medical profession.

At the Salvation Colony he set up a little laboratory for the business. He called the room the holy of holies. The bogus money was put into ALCA account under the guise of aid from the American Council of Churches. Before his suicide he would drag his small engraving plant and dump into a pit latrine. After his death we the members of the inner circle of **The Colony** would discover tins of powder and dyes, and mercury and half-engraved notes in his secret laboratory. We would conceal this part of our discovery from curious outsiders, from the press, from concerned relatives. But the police, discovering some bundles of the undeposited counterfeit notes, would make a good harvest, touch the loose ones, smell them and then exclaim gleefully:

"How could we have caught a man like this when his own notes are even better than the original?"

"Yes we would. But for now, he would respond to every question the way he had thought us to respond - honestly, knowing that there was nothing we would do to him.

Chapter Thirty-Three

Dennis Nunqam Ndendemajem

I did," he confessed his deed with the bank cashier. Shrapnell noticed with an embarrassed smile the progressive disappearance of respect in my attitude towards him. I had begun by addressing him "Our Father." Then as the interrogation proceeded in that strange manner I found myself addressing him "Reverend Pastor Sixtus Shrapnell", and finally " **You**." He saw immediately that he would never mean the same to us again. He saw his mission to Africa end in humiliation.

His candour both frightened and disarmed us. I held down my head for a long time and then raised it and looked round. I then dried my watery eyes with the back of my right hand and exhaled a deep sigh of resignation.

"Brethren," I began again. "You remembered that when you came in I said I suspected that somebody had infiltrated our stronghold and was using you to make a fool of me?"

I looked wrathfully into the eyes of his brethren. Tears suddenly rose to my tired eyes and I closed them for a while with a sigh. In the instant I thought of Dr Essemo, of Manda, of Cosmas, of my uncle, Pa Andre, of Joachim, of Dr. Eshuonti, and of everybody on whom I had turned my back to chase this shadow. It hurt.

"This is not infiltration, Pastor," I pointed out. "You opened this colony to save and to serve us. We have never ceased to show our gratitude towards you. You have been our way. If therefore we learn of something about your person which in our considered opinion we find detrimental to the well-being of this colony, we think it is our obligation to talk to you about it. We are only shocked by the answers you have given. If the answers you have given are actually true, then we are sincerely shocked. I for one, I do not know how I shall ever be able to hold up my head again."

"Brethren,"

"Pastor," we answered, staring unblinkingly into his eyes.

"Today may be the last day. Matthew 10 verse 22 says rightly: *"And you will be hated by all for My name's sake. But he who endures to the end will be saved."*

"At that so-called press conference when it comes if you shall rise to ask me those questions, I shall give you those very same answers."

A chill traversed my spine, and that of the others no less. There was a sudden silence in the room and we were all struck with much shame.

"What?" we shouted.

"Oh yes," Shrapnell put in remorselessly. "I shall answer precisely so. Speak the truth and speak it ever. He that hides the wrong he does, does the wrong thing still. And then I shall ask the world one question: do these answers mean that I led you to Satan and not to God?"

There was silence.

"Even as he was about to die,' he began looking round with haggard eyes, "Christ shared his last meal and drink with his followers. Silver and gold have I not, but such as I have give I thee in the name of Jesus Christ of Nazareth. Take your cups and drink with me." He lifted his coke to his lips. With a face that had crumbled into dissipated and exhausted lines, I rose and walked up to the table and with something like an exaggerated air of meekness, took up the cup of the drink he had personally served and said:

"Pastor, I served you this drink. You have always been our way, our resurrection and life. Lead us by tasting of this drink first." We had all sensed that there was something the matter with the drink. We all stared at him with a rising of the loathing which only a man can feel who has trapped his foe, a loathing which was actually physical as at the approach of some noisome and disgusting creature, full of venom and noxiousness.

We all rose and surrounded Shrapnell like ravenous wolves, and in a manner which implied that if he did not drink on his own we would force it down his throat.

Shrapnell seized the cup and, opening his mouth gulped down everything. But as soon as he licked his lips we noticed him grimace and sink back into his chair.

"There will be no press conference tomorrow," he said wrinkling his exhausted brow. There was a nervelessness in his voice and body which was pathetic, a terrifying numbness. "Tomorrow is now," he said down his throat. Then from nowhere his anger became directed against the black race. "A pack of unredeemable monkeys," he said.

I heard the words from a tremendous distance so that I had a hollow but murderous echo in his ears.

We saw him grip his belly and scream as if he had swallowed a dozen needles. I bent over him and held his hand. Shrapnell trembled for two minutes like a man in the grip of high fever and sank back, dead. I looked at the others, then at Shrapnell, then at the drinks we had been served, and then at the cup from which Shrapnell had just drunk. It would be established within an hour that Shrapnell had drunk poison, made from the bile of a python, and that he had hoped to poison us his faithful followers and die with us.

With our breasts simmering with a poisonous hatred, disappointment and repulsion, the twelve of us men left him lying in his chair and locked the door behind us.

Chapter Thirty-Four

Cosmas Mfetebeunu, Istromo Ngiawa

We did not even wait for Dennis to send for us. We knew that if Dennis and his fellows had confronted Shrapnell already, he would be already so dispirited that he would not have the strength to send us away. When we came to the gate it was locked. We sent for Dennis.

Dennis did not come alone, he was accompanied by six other persons including a woman. They were all looking gloomy. Dennis' once so lively appearance had suddenly assumed grave and drawn features. He looked distant in thought, with his face looking thin and rather hollow.

Bubbling with confidence in our own triumph, we had come expecting to be congratulated for saving the inmates from shame.

"Moyo Dennis," I called ingratiatingly. "You met with him?"

"We met with him," Dennis said, with a sickening of the heart and an unredeemed dreariness of thought which made him seem too dead to act positively. The heat was unbearably oppressive. Dennis pulled out a handkerchief from his pocket and wiped the sweat from his face.

"And how did it go? Did you ask him the questions?"

Dennis nodded, not a muscle moved on his petrified face.

"And how did he respond?"

Dennis smiled and raised his eyes to the sky, his lips contorting in a pitiful grimace. It had been a dull rather dark day with black cumulus clouds hanging oppressively and threatening with rain. Now despite the heat, thick heavy

203

rain clouds were dragging themselves across towards the west, indicating the approach of devastating rain.

"No comment," Dennis said just as Pastor Shrapnell said when we came to interview him the second time. With his confidence in the innate decency of man having been shaken, I could sense his mind slipping fast back into gloom and feverish despondency again. "Some truths are too bad to be known," Dennis said. "They are worse than lies. They wound. They really wound," he said as he walked away.

"Mr. Dennis, please," my pal Cosmas called after him. One of the persons who had come with Dennis to the gate persuaded him to come back and answer us. Dennis turned and came back.

"Will there be a press conference or not?" we asked.

"There will be a press conference," he said with unyielding obstinacy.

"Can we talk to Pastor Shrapnell?"

"You cannot talk to him," he said gravely.

"Why can't we talk to him?" I persisted.

"Because he is dead," Dennis said.

I looked at Istromo and he too looked at me, perplexed. I thought I did not hear him well.

"Assuming that Pastor Shrapnell is dead," I began, "who then shall call the press conference?"

"I shall call the press conference," Dennis said, his frail frame deeply shakened and on the point of an emotional breakdown.

There was a long silence.

"But Mr. Dennis, we don't understand," Cosmas cut in. "If as you say, Pastor Shrapnell is dead, then that is the end of **The Colony**..."

"It is not the end of **The Colony**," Dennis said resolutely. "God has not died with Shrapnell. So long as there is God, **The Colony** will exist..."

"How will you find money to run it?"

"God will provide. Prayer is the key."

Epilogue

There was no press conference, at least not in the officially arranged manner. Every morning, within living memory, a bell was rung at the entrance into **The Colony**. Every morning at five o'clock, one of the twelve keepers rang it. By seven o'clock the next morning, nobody remembered having heard the bell, meaning that there was no prayer session which usually preceded manual labour.

At 8 o'clock when they were supposed to have assembled for breakfast, the bell rang. The twelve Keepers appeared on the stage from which Our Father usually said the grace before meals. As if in prayer, they bowed their heads. Brother Dennis stepped in front to speak, to give the programme of the day.

"Dearest brethren," he began most emotionally. "I have bad news for you. The long-awaited press conference between Our Father, Reverend Pastor Sixtus Shrapnell, will no longer take place."

He paused to take in the reaction of the group. There was silence because everybody expected an explanation.

"Because why?" somebody asked furiously.

"Because Pastor Shrapnell is dead," Dennis nodded grimly and then added: "he took away his own life." There was a long silence. For the two years or so that Dennis had lived in **The Colony** they had been trained to look on death as the most ordinary phenomenon in human existence. Colonists were trained not to show sorrow of any sort to any loss. It had thus become a way of life with them. "Were they now to contradict that philosophy?

205

"It may be possible that the press is right, and that Reverend Pastor Sixtus Shrapnell did some of the things, or even all the things of which he was being accused. But he is no more, and so we shall never really know the truth. Maybe the fact that he has killed himself proves that he knew he was guilty. That too, we cannot answer. But let me ask you this: did your encounter with Reverend Pastor Sixtus Shrapnell change your life or not?"

"It changed our lives," a volley of voices answered.

"It changed mine too," Dennis said looking unseeingly in the direction of Cosmas and Istromo who had come ready to take him home. He looked round the madding crowd of freaks, the lame, the blind, the good, the bad, the ugly, the hungry, the weak, the strong, the fat, the thin. And then he asked: "Did he lead you to God or to Satan?"

"He led us to God," they shouted back.

"So, brethren, for better or for worse, **The Colony** lives on. We have done as he said up to now. Let us not do as he has done."